Tempest at the Sunsphere

David H—
8-16-08

Tempest at the Sunsphere

A NOVEL

David Hunter

Tellico Books
Oak Ridge, Tennessee

Tellico Books is an imprint
of the Iris Publishing Group, Inc

Cover Photo and Book Design: Robert B. Cumming, Jr.

Library of Congress Cataloging-in-Publication Data

Hunter, David, 1947-
Tempest at the sunsphere : a novel / David Hunter.
p. cm.
Includes bibliographical references and index.
ISBN 978-1-60454-001-7 (pbk. : alk. paper)
1. Police—Tennessee—Fiction. 2. Knoxville (Tenn.)—Fiction. I. Title.
PS3558.U46964T46 2008
813'.54—dc22

2008021687

This book is dedicated to the women who have encouraged, nagged, criticized and corrected me, turning out a fair writer in the process: Helen Hunter, Cheryl Krooss Hunter, Irene Maxwell, and Shelia Law.

Prologue

The 1982 World's Fair was supposed to be the biggest thing that ever happened in Knoxville, Tennessee. That is debatable, but it brought more than eleven million people from all over the globe to the growing city overlooking the Tennessee River.

Most visitors were tourists who went back home after sampling international cuisine and visiting the various pavilions. Some were con men and thieves of whom a few stayed in the prison system. Still others were homeless and found Knoxville very accommodating.

The fair was constructed on a 70-acre site between downtown Knoxville and the University of Tennessee. The most popular exhibits at the fair were those by China, Peru and Egypt. The Peruvian exhibit featured a mummy which was unwrapped and studied at the fair. The Egyptian exhibit featured ancient artifacts valued at over thirty million dollars.

Hungary's giant Rubik's cube may have been the most memorable thing about that World's Fair. The taste of World's Fair Beer may have been the most forgettable. Issued in several color editions, the cans were projected to become the most valuable souvenir, but twenty-five years later, you still can't give it away.

For many in Knoxville, the 1982 World's Fair was vindication from a comment by a *Wall Street Journal* reporter who allegedly had once referred to Knoxville as a "scruffy little city on the banks of the Tennessee River." Signs went up during the fair that said: "The scruffy little city did it!" Most Knoxvillians didn't know it, nor would they have cared what some New York reporter had said.

The theme of that fair was: *Energy Turns the World*, and the Sunsphere was the centerpiece. As the name implies, it is essentially a majestic glass ball, with five levels, perched on a metal frame. The glass panels are layered in 24-karat gold dust. It peaks at two-hundred and sixty-six-feet, has a volume of 203,689 cubic feet and a surface area of 16,742 square feet.

When the fair opened, it cost two dollars to take the elevator to its observation deck of the Sunsphere. The tower served as a restaurant and featured food items such as the *Sunburger* and a drink called the *Sunburst.*

The promoters of the World's Fair had hoped it would become as famous as the Seattle Space Needle, but it didn't. However, Bart, from *The Simpsons* television show, *did* visit the Sunsphere in one episode.

Throughout most of its history, the Sunsphere has languished as an iconic architectural curiosity, though at times open to the public in one guise or another. At the moment, the observation deck is open. Tomorrow that may change again.

The prospect of millions of visitors had touched off a deluge of greed in 1980 and 1981 that may have exceeded any such period in Knoxville's history. Everyone with a spare room saw dollar signs.

Poor people within a ten mile radius of downtown were kicked out of their apartments and rental housing because landlords intended to get rich renting by the week at astronomical prices.

Even the charitable downtown Freemasons got caught up in the greed and rented out their parking lot, supposedly for daytime only. But it was hard to control visitors. Some downtown members of that fraternity moved to outlying Masonic lodges and never returned.

Trailer parks were opened for the overflow crowds that never materialized and the owners went bankrupt before the fair ended.

The financial windfall had been projected to be five million dollars or more, but according to one source, the profit came to fifty-seven dollars. It was generally agreed that Knoxville only broke even on its world's fair.

Local police officers became familiar with the World's Fair Park because security was much in demand. A quarter of a century after the fair, one police officer who had banked a lot of money keeping order there, made a final visit to the Sunsphere.

One

My name is Shiloh Tempest. My friends call me "Shy." Since my mother died, only Jennifer, my in-house attorney and *compañera* of almost twenty years, calls me Shiloh.

I'm Chief of Detectives with the Knox County Sheriff's Office in Knoxville, Tennessee, which is around a hundred-fifty-miles east of the more famous and larger city of Nashville.

K-Town, as truckers call Knoxville, is just thirty miles or so west of Gatlinburg and Pigeon Forge, which are smaller but also more famous because of the Smoky Mountains and Dolly Parton who was born in Sevier County where they are located.

Historically speaking, I am probably the unhealthiest chief deputy who ever held the position — I have a defibrillator in my chest to keep the heart beating — and certainly the only chief of detectives in the Knox County who ever shot his predecessor to death since the department was founded in 1792.

The former chief of detectives was a predator who went off the reservation and I happened to be the man who discovered it. We didn't have a shootout at high noon but we did have one just after nine o'clock one evening in the squad room of the sheriff's office, where he had showed up to slit my throat — but that's a story for another day.

On a recent warm night in June, I went to the World's Fair Park because a body had been found at the foot of the Sunsphere, which was the centerpiece for the 1982 Knoxville World's Fair.

The World's Fair Park, or what's left of it, is in the jurisdiction of the Knoxville Police Department, but the body of the man found at the foot of the Sunsphere was Jerry Carpenter, an old cop friend of mine and a former KPD officer.

I had no official reason to be there. I was essentially snooping because I could.

Finding an out-of-the-way parking spot, I pulled my cruiser to the side of the street. It's a beat up old Ford. My predecessor had driven a brand new Chevy, but I'm of the opinion that the people who do the real police work should have the best cars.

A husky, young KPD patrol officer stepped forward as I walked under the Clinch Avenue viaduct, but I showed him my identification and seven-pointed star and he said, "Go on in, Chief."

The brass were clustered up together by the small man-made lake, with the Amphitheater in the background, so I walked over as a courtesy to let them know I was on the scene.

Jim "Dog" Jolsen, my counterpart at the Knoxville Police Department saw me and spoke: "As I live and breathe, it's Shy Tempest, the cop who stirs up a storm wherever he goes."

Jim is what a fiction writer might describe as blade-thin. Medium height, short gray hair and a crease in his trousers, no matter what the hour. He was the same way as a patrol officer, always neatly turned out, every hair in place. A thin, riverboat gambler mustache was his only personal statement.

"Who called you, Shy?" His worn cop's face said what his voice would never say. He knew how close Jerry and I had been at one time.

"If I gave you my source, I'd have to kill you, Dog. What happened to Jerry?"

"He was hit hard in the back of the head, but it probably didn't kill him. He was gutted, Shy. Somebody gutted Jerry the way you'd gut a deer."

"Does it look like rage or ritual?"

"We don't know yet, Shy. He's a mess. I don't need to tell you that this information is confidential."

"Of course, Dog. Any idea why he was here?"

"Not a clue, Shy. As far as I know, he did his drinking out in North Knox County where he lived after he left the department.

We sent a car by and his old pickup truck is parked in front of that dump where he lived on Clinton Highway."

Frank Hodge, the KPD Chief of Police was staring at me from the other side of the cluster of brass. A beefy man with a drunk's florid complexion, Hodge and I had never been friends.

When Hodge saw that I had noticed him, he spoke. "Your buddy, Jerry, finally ended up dead, just the way I expected he would when he went bad back in 1989. Are you here to pay your respects or looking for material for your next novel?"

"Actually, Chief Hodge, we *all* end up dead. But to answer your question, my next novel will be about a busted-up cop who got addicted to painkillers and was drummed out, rather than treated, by an office eunuch who had sucked his way into the chief's job. No, wait, that's a *true* story."

"Whatever your business is, Tempest, get it done and move on," Hodge said, his face flushing. "You're inside a KPD crime scene."

"Your KPD crime scene is inside the jurisdiction of the Knox County Sheriff's Office, for which I am a deputy chief, but I'm not going to take over the investigation, unless you think I should."

Hodge's already flushed face went a deeper, almost maroon shade, but he said nothing else. Male rhinos seldom charge each other.

Dog smiled and said in a low voice, "You can get his back up better than anyone I know, Shy. You want to look at Jerry before we move him?"

"I don't want to cause you any trouble with your boss, Dog."

"Trouble, my ass! I got my twenty-five in, Shy. I can walk tomorrow with a nice pension. Come on."

The yellow and black "Do Not Cross" police tape was draped over the orange safety net that surrounded the area at the bottom of the Sunsphere where construction crews were doing renovations.

"The construction barrier was trampled down when the homeless guy got here and saw Jerry's body. The forensics people are going to have an overabundance of cigarette butts, gum wrappers and God knows what else," Dog said.

Jerry's body was covered by a sheet and Dog pulled it back to reveal his face. He had died in agony, his eyes staring at whoever had killed him. He was clean-shaven, which was unusual in the latter part of his life. Usually he had a couple of day's growth between times he remembered to shave. "You want to see the damage, Shy?"

"No thanks, I'll wait on the autopsy report." I've always had a weak stomach, which was why I never worked homicide. "You'll keep me updated won't you, Dog. Here's a card with my cell number."

"I'll do better than that, Shy." He turned to a couple of officers in suits standing to the side, as forensics shot pictures and examined the pavement around the body and the pool of blood it lay in. "Abernathy and Claiborne, come over here."

The two men walked over without hesitation. One was tall and black with a shaved head, the other was shorter, more compact and had neatly combed blond hair. Both looked to be in their early thirties.

"Tom Abernathy and Rex Claiborne, also known as the Salt and Pepper team," nodding at each as he spoke. "You two guys know Chief Shy Tempest? Well *now* you do. I want you to keep him updated on this case. He and Jerry were old buddies from their narcotics days."

"Nice to meet you," Abernathy's large black hand swallowed my pale, stubby one in a firm shake. "I've read your books."

Claiborne also extended his hand, but his grip was damp and limp. "Nice to meet you, Chief Tempest."

I handed each of them a card as Dog lowered his voice. "Just don't let Hodge know you're talking to Shy. He doesn't like Shy for the same reason a lapdog dislikes a wolf."

"Gotcha covered, Chief," Abernathy said.

"You have any thoughts on this, Chief Tempest?" the blond Claiborne asked.

"Yes, but it never pays to let speculation enter an investigation too early. Just follow the leads and they'll take you where you need to go."

The sun was barely coming up as I pulled into my driveway and saw that lights were on inside. I pushed the remote attached to my sun visor and the garage door opened.

I left the cruiser parked outside, walked into the garage and hit the button on the wall to close it. I opened the door into our kitchen and saw my beautiful Colombian *compañera*, Jennifer, sitting at the kitchen table, drinking coffee and reading the newspaper.

"You're up early," I said, leaning over to kiss her on the lips. Jen looks better than most women in a housecoat and no makeup than they do dressed for a ball.

When she walks into a courtroom, people take deep breaths. She's easily the most beautiful lawyer in the state — maybe in the country. The *real* shock for the opposition comes when they discover that her brains exceed her beauty.

"Who called this morning and dragged you away?" she asked.

"Old KPD friend named Jameson. Jerry Carpenter's body was found at the foot of the Sunsphere. Somebody hit him in the head and disemboweled him."

"Oh God, what a horrible way to die! Does anyone know why he might have been at the Sunsphere?"

"Not yet, but you know how Jerry was when he was doing painkillers and drinking at the same time. Anybody he knew could talk him into going anywhere," I said.

"I was going to ask a favor, but my problem seems small now. How do *you* feel? I've never had a close friend die violently, and I can't imagine it."

"You know how it is, Jen. Cops compartmentalize things. It's all in there, every horrible thing I've ever seen, waiting to spill out. I suppose I should cry or something, but I've been waiting for years now for the call telling me Jerry is dead. It's not a big surprise.

"What was the favor you needed?"

"I've been trying to get a subpoena served on one Jorge Chávez. He can clear my client of a rape charge, but he's dropped off the radar."

"Do you have his sheet and picture?"

"Yes, I do." She handed me a local arrest sheet on him with his mug shot copied in black and white.

"This guy's no angel," I said. "Two public intoxications and one Schedule VI bust for selling weed."

"No, he *isn't* and neither is my client, but my client isn't a rapist and Jorge Chávez was with him the night the rape occurred, all the way across town."

"All right, I'll see what I can do today. I'm going to get a shower and go on to work."

"You need your rest, Shiloh. Your cardiologist keeps telling you that."

"I had four hours, Jen. Besides, I've got my own defibrillator. If my heart tries to stop, it will start me back up again."

"Shiloh, what *are* we going to do with you?"

I showered and headed to the City-County building.

Thirty minutes later, I got off the elevator on the mezzanine and stopped by the Criminal Court Clerk's office to pick up a subpoena on Jorge Chávez. I was pretty sure I could locate him and have a nice lunch at the same time.

Two levels down, I went by the sheriff's department records section to pick up my mail and messages. The Sheriff came out of his office and spotted me as I started back to the elevators.

"Shy, if you have a minute, I'd like to speak with you." Sam Renfro hadn't been sheriff long. He had been appointed to fill out the term of the previous sheriff, who had been caught with his hand, all the way up to the elbow, in the county cash box.

When Sam was appointed sheriff by the Knox County Commission to fill out the term of Jack Smotherman, he had a murder case that was nearly two years old. He brought me in as a consultant to look at the case with fresh eyes.

When it turned out that the chief of detectives *was* the murderer, which led to the shooting in the squad room, Sam asked me to stay on as chief of detectives for a while.

In the sheriff's office, he closed the door behind us. Sam is about fifty, nine years younger than I am. He dresses in tailored suits and coordinates his colors.

Myself, I wear solid colored suits, plaid shirts and solid colored ties to match. But when Sam and I worked narcotics and criminal intelligence, nobody could look more street than he did. It's a chameleon-like quality he has.

Once, when he came to work wearing saddle oxfords, I made a comment about them. He had stopped, looked directly at me and asked, "Do you have any idea how big a set of *cojones* I must have to wear these shoes around cops?"

There was no quick reply, so he had the last word.

"What's up, Hoss? I didn't see your car in the parking bay and thought you weren't here. Your car in the shop?"

"Sam, my car is in the main parking garage where it always is."

"The eternal egalitarian, Shy. That's what you are. If you feel better driving an old cruiser than a new one, be my guest. But you're a deputy chief and the chief of detectives. Use your parking spot. It's *not* a suggestion. Besides, you've got a bionic heart and I want you around for a few years."

"All right, Sam. I'll park in the bay. Did you call me in just to discuss where I park?"

"No, Frank Hodge called first thing this morning and said you were interfering in a KPD investigation."

"That's a lie. I was there but I didn't get in the way. Jerry Carpenter was murdered last night. Somebody gutted him like a deer."

"Hodge didn't mention that."

"No, he wouldn't. Hodge is the one who drummed him out

of KPD instead of sending him to rehab. Jerry was a good cop and a brave man."

"That he was, Shy. But Frank Hodge, asshole that he is, still runs the Knoxville Police Department and I don't want a pissing contest with him. I'm not going to tell you to stay away from the investigation, because I know you won't. Try to keep the friction to a minimum, okay?"

"I'll try to avoid Hodge," I said.

"Good. How's that lovely Latina lawyer you should have married years ago? I never understood what she sees in a scarred, old dog like you."

"Neither do I, Sam. Neither do I. As for *why* we're not married, that's her choice."

Two

Traffic was unusually light at noon when I left my office. I headed north on I-75 in an unmarked, new Chevrolet sedan. Sam had sent the fleet manager to find my old cruiser and make it presentable.

After the deed was done, the fleet manager called and told me I would temporarily be driving the car parked in the bay next to the sheriff's spot. He asked what color I wanted on the old cruiser and I told him maroon because I didn't think he would do it.

I turned on to Merchant Drive. A couple of blocks down, I pulled into the parking lot of the Nogales Restaurant where I often eat lunch. There are a host of Mexican restaurants in Knoxville these days — ranging from Tex-Mex chains catering to gringo ideas of what Mexicans eat — to a few like Nogales that are authentic Mexican fare.

When I was growing up, Mexicans were those guys who wore sombreros and serapes and took siestas every afternoon. By the time I was in my late thirties, Upper East Tennessee, home to canning factories was rife with immigrants from Mexico, Ecuador, Panama and many other countries south of the border, coming in to do seasonal work.

Some of them stayed. I talked to the wife of the first Latino police officer in Johnson City, Tennessee. Whatever the nationality of the parents, the children are Americans, but Americans who maintain the culture of their parents to some degree.

To accommodate the Latin immigrants, restaurants sprang up. The tide of those with Spanish names moved across the state, and by the time it reached Knoxville, those calling themselves *conservatives* had fixated on immigrants — here illegally or not — as the cause of the economic woes besetting the country.

Almost overnight, it seemed, there were dark-skinned men, many short and stocky, and beautiful women with dark hair and eyes, standing in the lines at department stores and supermarkets, trying to buy into the American dream.

Some people did their best to turn that dream into a nightmare. But the Latin tide kept coming and most brought a work ethic that shamed their pale predecessors.

I walked into the Nogales Restaurant and smelled a delicious mélange of spices.

"*Hola*, Shy. You alone today?" Juan Dominga, the owner said.

"*Hola*, Juan. Can you join me for a few minutes?"

"Sure, you want the usual?"

"Yes, please." Juan has been in Tennessee for twenty years, by way of Texas. His English is better than mine.

"Hey," Juan yelled at one of the waiters, "two chiles rellenos, a tamale and a beef burrito over at my table, and a diet cola."

"So, Shy, what's on your mind today?" Juan asked as we sat down in a corner booth, which he only allowed to be used by customers when the place was packed. Juan is a hefty man with a big belly and he had the contractors make the corner booth with extra room.

"First thing is the food, especially the chiles rellenos. The other thing is, I'm trying to locate this man." I took the folded rap sheet with Chávez's picture and slid it across the table.

Juan unfolded it and studied it carefully. "Shy, this isn't an *inmigración* matter is it? I don't care about putting away criminals, but you know how I feel about *la migra*," he said, using Spanish slang for immigration.

"*Amigo*, you know better than that." In times past, I had intervened on behalf of his undocumented employees when they were stopped by other cops — assuming they weren't committing genuine crimes.

"Just asking. You know, of course, that I don't know *every* Mexican in Knox County," Juan said with a wry smile.

"Sí, mi amigo. Lo sé."

"Just checking, Shy, to make sure you remember," he said with a grin. "Jorge is working in the kitchen at the Mexicali Cantina on Chapman Highway."

"Thank you," I said, just as the waiter put down my food on dishes hot enough to burn the unsuspecting.

"So, Shy, how is Jennifer *la bella*?"

"She's good, Juan. Working too many *pro bono* cases, but good."

"You're looking a lot better now that the two of you are back together, Shy."

"Does *everyone* know we were separated, Juan?"

"*Hombre*, your friends knew."

In a fit of depression, I had moved out of our house because I thought it would be the best for my Jennifer. She had never agreed and stuck with me through a really bad patch.

"Besides, word gets around when a beautiful Latina doesn't like spicy Mexican food, you know," Juan said.

"Give her a break, Juan. She's Colombian, not Mexican. Now you're the one lumping all Latins into the same ethnic group."

"Touché!"

I took my first bite of the chile relleno and it was still almost too hot to chew. Juan and I sat chatting as I ate. I was having my last bite of burrito when my cell phone rang.

"Excuse me, Juan." I opened the flip-top phone. "Hello?"

"Chief Tempest, this is Detective Abernathy. We're getting ready to toss Jerry Carpenter's apartment. I thought you might want to be there."

"I appreciate that, Detective. I can be there in fifteen minutes."

"Muy bueno todo, mi amigo. La cuenta, por favor, I said."

"My friends don't get checks here, Shy."

"In that case, Juan, a nice tip for the waiter and cooks." I put a twenty on the table and left before he could protest. It is an ongoing matter between us, the matter of free meals. Once he lumbered out to the parking lot and threw my money through my open car window.

Sometimes he wins, sometimes I win. Either way, I am the beneficiary.

Tom Abernathy and Rex Claiborne were already there when I arrived, waiting outside. The weather was warm, but they were both in suits and ties, as is the custom at KPD for all detectives not undercover.

Jerry had lived in a single room in what had once been a Clinton Highway motel when 25W was the main highway north, before I-75 changed that. A few struggled all the way into the 1980s, but now all of them are either strip malls or efficiency apartments.

"Thanks for calling, Abernathy. Good to see both of you."

They responded cordially, but Abernathy with more enthusiasm than the pale blond Claiborne. Using a passkey they had gotten from the landlord, we entered the one-room apartment where Jerry Carpenter had spent the last ten years of his life.

"He didn't leave much behind for his family," Abernathy said as we surveyed the room. The drapes were closed and the room was dim until Claiborne switched on the light.

"The only family he had left was an ex-wife he hadn't seen in years," I said.

There was a small television, a CD video player, a bed, a cluttered dresser, one chair and a small refrigerator. Clothes were hanging from a free-standing metal rack. At the front of the rack was a leather jacket and a motorcycle helmet hanging by the chin strap that said, "Blue Hawk" on the side.

"I didn't know Carpenter was ever a motor man," Abernathy said.

"Yep, he was a Blue Hawk," I said. "He was on a department motorcycle when he got busted up so badly. He went back to work, but he never got off the pain pills."

"Rehab didn't take, huh?" Claiborne said.

"He was never given the *option* of rehab. An assistant chief named Frank Hodge had him drummed out of the department."

"What was Hodge's beef with Carpenter?" Abernathy asked.

"Carpenter held Hodge in contempt because he never worked the streets," I answered.

"Damn, look at all those pill bottles," Claiborne said.

"In addition to the bad joints, Jerry had other medical problems," I said.

Claiborne walked across the room and picked up a plastic baggie with white powder in it. Whatever this is, it ain't prescription," he said.

Abernathy took the baggie with the white powder from his partner's hand, stepped into the small bathroom and shook it out into the toilet. He flushed it and said: "No use smearing a dead cop."

"Look," Claiborne said, "the only picture in here is of Jerry and a good looking blonde. Looks like a high school prom picture. You know this woman, Chief?"

I examined the picture closely. It was imprinted at the bottom in a faded gold lettering, "Carter High School, Senior Class of 1979."

"No, I don't recognize her, but she must have been special to Jerry."

"Chief, it looks like Carpenter was going to the University of Tennessee. Here's an anthropology textbook and a notebook. The notebook says at the top of the first page, 'Professor Wyatt.' Did you know Carpenter was a student?"

"No, but then Jerry kept things pretty much to himself when he was sober. And he was always sober when he called me to have lunch with him."

Before Abernathy could say anything else, his cell phone gave a bugle call. Individual tastes vary, I suppose. My cell phone plays "The Sting." He stepped outside the room to take the call.

Claiborne and I stood in an uncomfortable silence until he came back in.

"This gets curiouser and curiouser," Abernathy said.

"Tell us about it," I said.

"Carpenter had a fragment of obsidian embedded in his skull and his heart is missing. This is beginning to read like fiction."

"What the hell is *obsidian?*" Claiborne asked.

"It's a form of volcanic glass," I said. "It makes an excellent cutting blade. In fact, I think some surgical scalpels are still made of it."

"There's more," Abernathy said, "and forensics called while I was talking to the medical examiner's office. The fragments of black stuff they picked up near Carpenter's body were charcoal, the run-of-the mill stuff that's used in charcoal grills."

"You're right, Abernathy. It does get curiouser and curiouser."

"Where the hell do the two of you get that word?" Claiborne asked. "Both of you must be university geeks. I just have an associates degree in criminal justice, but I know when somebody's talking over my head."

"It's from *Alice in Wonderland*," I told him. "And I never went to college at all."

"Never read it," Claiborne said.

Three

After I left Abernathy and Claiborne at Jerry's apartment, I drove north on Clinton Highway, feeling a little guilty about where I was heading. After all, it was their case and they had been nice enough to keep me updated. But where I was going, nobody would talk to them.

I passed the old Airplane Filling Station — that's what they were called before they became *service* stations — where long lines of cars once waited to gas up and have their pictures made on the way to points north or points south. It had still been a tourist attraction when I was a small child. It was a one of a kind place like you don't see any longer because of the Interstate system.

The fuselage of the airplane replica had served as the office for a Texaco station with restrooms in the back, out of sight. I'm told it was built to look like a Curtis Robin aircraft, but I really don't know. Built around 1930 by a couple of brothers named Nickle, it has been a package store, produce market and used car lot through years. It's now on the National Register of Historic Places and a non-profit group is working to restore it.

My destination was a bar that had only been around since the 1980s, though it had been called many other names before nude dance pioneer Sammy Sullivan had opened up as Sammy's Place. He was an old-time operator who preferred putting one over on the cops to making money. I had been a thorn in his side when I was a patrol officer.

The strip joint was in an old block building and the Sammy's Place sign was peeling. I got out and opened the door to the foyer. Behind a Plexiglas window with a slot for money to be passed in, sat Sammy himself. He had to be at least eighty, but still kept his silver hair regularly styled.

"Let me in, you old reprobate," I said.

"It's the no-neck cop back to harass poor old Sammy," he said, throwing the electronic switch to unlock the inner door.

"Poor old Sammy, my ass! You've gotten filthy rich catering to human weakness."

"Somebody will always do that, Shiloh. Might as well be me." Our relationship had improved a lot since I left patrol. In fact, he was one of my regular informants, which would have shocked most people who knew him.

"Business or pleasure?" he asked, as a bored woman in her thirties gyrated onstage wearing only a g-string and transparent latex pasties. The latex is a technical compliance with an anti-nudity ordinance.

"Neither really, Sammy. It's not my case, but somebody killed Jerry Carpenter last night. I know he spent a lot of time here."

"I'm sorry to hear that," Sammy said. "Until a couple of months ago, he was here every night we were open. Since then, he's been here every night we're open except for Thursdays."

"What changed?"

"I don't know, but Sadie could probably tell you. Come on back, she just came in a few minutes ago. She's putting on her makeup."

"Is Sadie her stage name?"

"No, her stage name is Stormy. Her real name is Sadie Hyde. Come on, I'll introduce you."

Raymond led me to the dressing room and opened the door. A woman wearing only a pair of panties was sitting in front of a mirror over a counter that ran the length of the room.

She was a redhead, or at least her hair was dyed red, and she had obviously had surgery to augment her breasts, which is common in her line of work. Her nails were long and painted a jade green color.

"Sadie, this is Lieutenant... no, it's now *Chief* Shy Tempest. He's a county cop, but you can talk to him."

"All right," she said. "Come in and have a seat."

"I gotta cover the front, Chief, until my doorman gets here." Sammy closed the door and left.

I took a seat on one of the stools along the counter that served as a dresser for the dancers. Sadie made no effort to cover up but went on applying eyeliner.

"Sadie, I understand you're a friend of Jerry Carpenter's."

"We're friends. I got in a scrape with an outlaw biker a couple of years ago and Jerry took care of the problem for me. Sometimes, I go by and spend the night with him when we're both lonely."

"I hate to be the one to break the news, but Jerry was killed last night."

Tears sprang to her eyes but she strove valiantly not to let me see she was disturbed. "*So*? It's not like I'm his next of kin or anything."

"Sadie, he was my friend, too. For more than twenty-five years. He was murdered and mutilated. I can't get into details, but it was bad."

"What do you want to know?" she asked, visibly taking control of her breathing.

Sammy said he was here every night you were open until a couple of months ago, but something changed. Do you know what it was?"

"He was taking a class at UT on Thursdays. I think there was a new woman in his life, but he never told me who she was. I smelled her perfume in his bed. Jerry and I never questioned each other. We were just there when either of us needed company."

"When did you last see Jerry?

"Three or four days ago," she replied.

"Sadie, did you..." I was interrupted.

The door opened and a behemoth of a man was standing there. Three-hundred plus pounds and maybe six-six, his head was shaved, which added to the effect of making him look like the pinhead attraction from an old sideshow.

"This guy botherin' you, Sadie?"

Before she could speak, I did. "I'm a police officer and there's an interview in progress. Back out and close the door."

"I don't care *what* you are. I asked Sadie if you was botherin' her. That ain't allowed here. He took a step forward. I was sitting and knew I'd never get to my pistol in time if he charged me in the enclosed space.

"Tiny, that's enough!" Sadie said, walking to him and placing her hand on his chest. The green fingernails made it appear as if a spider had landed on his chest against the white shirt. "Sammy let him in. Now close the door before you get in trouble."

"You didn't scare me none," Tiny said. "Sadie, you need me, scream. He bothers you away from here, you got my cell number." He stepped back and shut the door.

"Who is the gentleman with the tiny head and the tiny brain?" I asked.

"His real name's Ralph Ogg, but we call him Tiny. He keeps order in here and he'd die for me or any of the other girls."

"Sadie, did you love Jerry?" I continued what I had been about to say when Tiny interrupted me.

"What's love have to do with anything? I didn't expect a house in the country with a picket fence, if that's what you mean." Sadie said.

"What does a house in the country and a picket fence have to do with love, Sadie?"

"Beats me," she said, regaining her composure. She stood up, stepped out of the panties and pulled on a g-string, then began to apply her transparent pasties.

"Do you need anything else or are you just enjoying the view?"

"No, I appreciate your time," I said, turning to leave.

"Have the funeral plans been made?" she asked before I was out the door.

"No, but I'd be glad to let you know when I find out."

"Just call and leave a message with Sammy. I'll be there if I have time."

While I was out, I decided to try and serve the subpoena on Jorge Chávez on the way back to my office. When I got off I-75 at

Western Avenue and turned right on Chapman Highway, I continued on south instead of hanging a left as I would have done on the way back to the City-County Building.

South Knoxville is cut off from the rest of the city by the Tennessee River and has kept its own distinctiveness. There are a lot of restaurants and little shops like the Book Eddy, which specializes in rare books. Mexicali Cantina is a couple of miles outside the city limits in a building once occupied by a fast food chain.

Inside the door, I stopped at the cash register. A pretty woman who looked to be about thirty and appeared to be Latina, smiled. "May I help you?" she asked in heavily accented English.

"*Necesito hablar con Jorge Chávez.*" I showed her my badge case with the seven-pointed star and ID card.

I saw the hesitation and the darting eyes and headed her off at the pass.

"*Señora,* I know he's here. *No soy de la migra. Quiero hablar con Jorge.*"

"*En la cocina,*" she said.

"*Gracias.*"

I walked to the kitchen and pushed through the swinging door. Jorge was chopping onions and looked up just as I entered the kitchen. He didn't wait to find out who I was. Jorge bolted out the back door.

By the time I got to the door, he was attempting to climb a kudzu covered embankment behind the restaurant, which sets in a spot cut out of the ridge behind the building "*Jorge, no soy de la migra!* I'm a police officer. I just need to talk to you. *No hay problema!*"

His attempts to climb the embankment failed. He ducked behind the dumpster, from which there was no way out.

"Jorge, you're *not* in trouble!" I shouted.

It was a total surprise when he leaned from behind the dumpster and fired a small pistol. I heard the buzz of the round and paint chips flew from the cinderblock building about two feet from me.

"Damn it," I yelled, drawing my pistol and taking cover behind an old Ford parked by the building. "Stop shooting! I only need to *talk* to you."

In answer, he fired two more rounds, one of which shattered the glass in the windshield of the old Ford. I rose up, peeked and scanned, then fired three rounds at him, and ducked again. A moment later Jorge began yelling in pain, staggered out from behind the dumpster and collapsed, dropping the pistol.

I approached, pistol at the ready and kicked what appeared to be a cheap .25 automatic away from him. His left arm was bleeding below the shoulder and he was babbling in Spanish faster than I could understand. I got on the radio and called for an ambulance and notified the department I had been involved in a shooting.

Jorge seemed unaware of my presence as I examined his arm and determined that he had only the one wound and that it was a through and through. He was lucky because cops don't train to wound. I had fired at the center of body mass but my aim was off. It always is when someone is trying to kill you.

I took off my necktie and used it to staunch the bleeding. I saw that several members of the restaurant staff had come outside, including the woman from the cash register.

"Why did he try to shoot me?" I asked her. "I told him I only needed to *talk* to him."

"His English is not so good," she said. "And his lawyer told him if he got in any more trouble with the law they'd take his green card and send him back to Mexico."

"He'd rather risk death than go back to Mexico?"

"Depends on what part of Mexico, I guess," she answered.

"Would you tell him an ambulance is on the way and his wound is minor."

The woman spoke to him in Spanish and the babbling stopped.

"What was he saying?" I asked.

"He was praying," she answered.

The ambulance arrived, followed by a young deputy sheriff I didn't know. As the ambulance crew examined Chávez, I laid out what had happened and he took notes.

"I'm going to follow him to the hospital. Secure the scene until major crimes gets here," I told the young officer.

"Internal affairs will be wanting to talk to you, Chief," the young cop said.

"Tell them they can catch up with me later..." I looked at his name tag "Officer Dotson."

On the way to the hospital, I called Jennifer's straight line at the law firm where she worked. "Hello?"

"Jen, can you meet me at University Hospital?"

"Are you hurt?" I could hear the catch in her voice.

"No, but I found Jorge Chávez and I need you to translate."

"Has he been in an accident?" she asked.

"Not exactly, Jen. I had to shoot him."

"My God, Shiloh. I just asked you to serve a subpoena, not *shoot* my witness."

"Jen, I didn't have much choice. But at least you'll know where to find him now. He'll be in jail for attempted murder and especially aggravated assault."

Four

Jerry Carpenter's funeral was not a large affair. Police were in the majority and three of us were watching the crowd. The Fraternal Order of Police picked up the tab for his funeral. He hadn't been to a meeting in nearly fifteen years, but he had kept up his dues.

I had taken his leather Blue Hawk jacket and helmet to the mortuary and he was wearing them. Frank Hodge had forbidden any KPD cruiser or motorcycle from taking part. Three or four of the older guys with whom he had worked had shown up in uniform because there wasn't much Hodge could do them; they had their pensions in already.

As a chaplain read scripture at the graveside, Abernathy whispered to me: "The guy with the Vandyke beard is Professor Tiberius Jonathon Wyatt. It was his class Carpenter was auditing at UT."

The man of whom Abernathy was speaking looked like a poser to me. A tall man dressed in a tweed jacket and corduroy trousers. His dark hair was overly-groomed and he had a British driving cap in his hand. I would have been willing to bet that there was a curved pipe in his coat pocket.

"Who's the good looking blonde beside the professor, wearing sunglasses?" I whispered.

"She's a professor, also. Her name's Deborah Clark, she teaches medieval studies. She and Wyatt have an informal get-together with a few students at his apartment once a week," Abernathy said in a barely audible voice.

"Let me guess, it's on Thursday evenings."

"How did you know that, Chief?"

"I ran into a stripper that Jerry knew really well. She told me Jerry had been taking a class, and going to a study group on Thursdays."

"Were you going to tell us about the stripper?"

"It was inconsequential. She didn't know any of his associates away from Sammy's Place."

"Oh yeah, Jerry's hangout. That was on our list of places to go when we could get around to it. I guess there's no need now."

"Detective Abernathy, I'm *not* trying to step on your case. It's just that I know a lot of people Jerry knew." As I spoke, I saw Sadie standing at the back of the crowd across from us.

"The redhead at the back of the crowd is Sadie Hyde, the one I talked to. Don't expect her to be cooperative. She talked to me because I was Jerry's friend."

"Maybe I'll wait, Chief."

"Do you have any objection to me talking to Wyatt and Clark now that you've already interviewed them?"

"Not at all," he whispered.

The chaplain stopped reading and the funeral home personnel lowered the casket into the ground. After a few respectful moments, the crowd began to disperse. I followed the two professors.

"Professor Clark," I called out.

They both stopped as I approached. "Professor Clark, I'm Shy Tempest, with the sheriff's office. I wonder if I might have a few words with you?"

"Detective, there's a time and a place for everything," the bearded professor said. "A funeral is *not* the proper place for an interview."

"Jon, just go on to the car. I'll be along in a minute. I know Mister Tempest," she said.

He walked away scowling, looking over his shoulder twice before he got to a green Austin-Healey Sprite with the top down. It's a very rare British sports car made in the late 1950s and early 1960s.

"Shiloh," she extended her hand, "forgive the white lie. Jon can be stuffy. I feel as if I know you because Jerry talked about you so often."

Up close, I could tell she was a rare natural blonde and that there was a lot of silver mixed in with the blond hair. Mental arithmetic told me she was forty-three. My eyes told me she had aged well. "He thought highly of you, also. He still had a picture of the two of you at the Carter High senior prom."

"Yes, I know that, Shiloh."

"So you've been in Jerry's apartment, then?"

"Yes, Shiloh. Jerry and I were lovers in high school and we became lovers again recently."

"Was a more permanent relationship in the works, Deborah?"

"Probably not. When we graduated from high school, the plan was to be together forever. Then Jerry joined the Army and I went to Europe to work on my masters. When I came back, he was married. When he got his divorce I was married.

"I hadn't seen him for years until I ran into him at Charlie Pepper's on the Cumberland strip a couple of months ago. We talked for hours. A few days later he was auditing one of Jon's classes because mine were full. He joined our informal Thursday study group. After the group, I'd sometimes follow Jerry home."

"So you were fond of him and he was fond of you, but a permanent relationship was *never* considered, Deborah?"

"Shy — may I call you that? Jerry did. He told me you had a way of cutting straight to the chase. He was right. I'm not an elitist. I loved Jerry, not the way I did when we were kids, but in a new way. It was Jerry who put the limits on our relationship. I think it was difficult for him to stay away from pills and booze, even for our one night a week together."

"Did Professor Wyatt know Jerry had set limits? He seems very possessive of you."

"No, I never discussed Jerry with him. Jon and I have been

friends for twenty years, even bedmates on occasion, but he has his life and I have mine."

"Well, Deborah, I'm sorry we had to meet under these circumstances. It's easy for me to see why Jerry found you so special."

"Shy Tempest! Jerry also told me that you have a way with women. You, sir, are a flatterer. I'm glad we finally met. I wish the circumstances had been different." She extended her hand and I grasped it firmly.

I watched her walk away and imagined Jerry sitting through lectures on ancient history to be with her. It couldn't have been really comfortable for either one of them, but old loves hang on long after the feasibility of some relationships depart.

"Chief Tempest!" Detective Abernathy called out my name.

I turned and he walked up beside me, a wry smile on his lips. "I should have taken my own advice. Sadie just told me to go screw myself because she doesn't talk to cops."

"Well, I'm convinced that Jerry's death had nothing to do with his strip club life, anyway. I think the answer may be tied up with the study group he joined a couple of months ago. You have anything on that yet?"

"Yeah, I have a list but Professor Wyatt said it's mostly kids interested in history. He told me that a male student in the group named Jedediah Osteen is unstable. He says the boy showed up once dressed as a Roman soldier and once as an Aztec warrior. I haven't been able to run down the Osteen boy yet."

"Sounds like a place to start," I said.

"Did you get anything interesting from Professor Clark?"

"Probably what she told you. She and Jerry were sleeping together on Thursdays after the study group met."

He stopped and stared at me. "She told you *that*?"

"Yes. She didn't tell you? Did you *ask* her?"

"No, she's such a class act..."

"And Jerry was a washed up, Clinton highway drunk." I said.

"Don't take it like *that*, Chief. They didn't move in the same social circles. That's all I meant. What made you even ask the question?"

"Well, Abernathy, there was something between them once. They went to the senior prom together. It seemed like a logical question to me."

"The girl in that picture at his place was Professor Clark?" Abernathy seemed stunned.

"Abernathy, you saw the picture, the same as I did. I thought you interviewed her."

"I did, Chief. I suppose I didn't ask the right questions."

"No, Abernathy, the problem was that you *assumed* things not in evidence, as my lawyer roommate would say. I've made a lot of assumptions in my time and at least half of them were wrong. You have to ask questions if you want answers."

"Chief Tempest, if you've already solved this case, will you just tell me so I don't keep blundering around?"

"No, Abernathy, I haven't solved it. But we will."

"By the way, Chief," Abernathy said. "Here's a list of the small items forensics picked up in the area around Jerry's body. Besides the charcoal, there was chewing gum, a dozen cigarette butts, a woman's false fingernail, a paper clip and candy wrapper among other items."

"It always hurts when the crime scene is accessible to the public," I said.

There are two things I've learned well in my lifetime: Life is what happens when you're making plans; and reality occurs when you're in a situation you don't like and can't escape. None of the so-called reality television problems are real. The people involved can leave whenever they want to. Reality isn't possible under those circumstances.

The few seconds before an automobile crash, being under fire and losing a loved one to death are real because you can't shut them off or hit the replay button. Still, Jerry Carpenter had done something few of us ever manage.

He had returned to the love of his life and she had returned to him. But the reality of nearly twenty years of drug and alcohol abuse had become more real than their love. They might have eventually worked through it, but the ultimate reality had shut Jerry down. I knew I wouldn't sleep well until his killer was brought to justice.

Abernathy and his partner had been good about keeping me updated on Jerry's case, but Pizza Hut doesn't tell Dominos everything, and it was *their* case. Cops want to solve their own cases. They'll take help but they always take more than they give. I know.

Back at the City-County Building I stopped off in records and waved to Tasha, the assistant records supervisor, whom I've known since she was a girl. Approaching forty, she is still strikingly beautiful and almost six-feet tall.

There had been a mild flirtation between us when she was very young but I don't take advantage of innocence. She thought I hadn't followed up because she was nearly six inches taller than I am. I just let her believe it.

"Hello, Short and Sexy," she said, walking to the counter.

"Hello, you gorgeous Amazon. How goes it?"

"Other than missing out on the man of my dreams, I'm good!"

"Well, you were always too much woman for me."

"How can I help you, Shy?"

"See if we have anything on Jedediah Osteen, approximate age of twenty and Tiberius Jonathon Wyatt, who will be in the neighborhood of fifty."

"Your wish is my command, O' Wise Chief of Detectives."

"You're pouring it on thick today, Tasha."

"What's shakin', Homes?" Sam Renfro had been walking by records.

"Not much, Sheriff. You watching the halls to see what time I come in?"

"Nope, just being sociable to an old comrade from the streets, Shiloh."

"I went to Jerry Carpenter's funeral this morning."

"I don't imagine there was a big crowd. People forget," Sam said.

"A few old cops. Frank Hodge forbade a police funeral — and a few people from Jerry's college study group."

"Jerry was going to college?"

"Actually, he was auditing a course to get close to his high school sweetheart. She's a professor at UT. Personally, I think Jerry's death was connected to that little study group he was in."

"If it's true, it's ironic. Look at everything Jerry survived as a cop. He was wilder than you were. I always figured that was why you were friends. I remember the time on Market Street when the drug dealer got the drop on you and Jerry.

"You two stepped apart and told him to decide who he liked the least, then to shoot because the other would draw and kill him before he got off the second round. He decided you were both crazy and threw down his gun."

"I guess we *all* were crazy, Sam. Sane people don't do the things we used to do."

"Catch you later, Shiloh. I have a budget meeting with county commission. Oh yeah try to be at least minimally polite to IAD."

"I'm always *minimally* polite to internal affairs, Sam."

After a couple of minutes, Tasha came back carrying copies of whatever she had found. "Good stuff here, Shy. This Osteen kid was arrested at the civic coliseum running naked across the floor — except for a sword and steel helmet. He was committed for observation that same night.

"This professor Wyatt was arrested for aggravated assault six years ago. We don't have a disposition, so it was probably dismissed or he was put on diversion."

"I wonder why he didn't have it expunged?"

"A lot of people think charges are automatically expunged if they aren't convicted," Tasha said. "What the average person doesn't know about the law would fill an encyclopedia."

"You're right about that, Tasha. If you'll excuse me, I'm going to check in with my office before I see the shooflies."

"They laid off an internal affairs officer when you retired the last time," Tasha said. They said it was because their workload decreased when you were gone."

"Tasha, you are a bundle of laughs," I said on my way out.

Sergeants Black and White were waiting on me when I knocked at their door. Troy Black and Terry White were the only officers in the history of the department to ever volunteer for internal affairs duty. "Mutt and Jeff" was one of the nicer epithets that had been hurled at them through the years.

Black was short and squat with a bald head and fringe on the sides and White was tall and lanky with a haircut reminiscent of the 1950 ducktail haircut, grease and all. Both were pushing fifty. The internal affairs office was one thing that had not changed in the twelve years I had been gone.

"Have a seat, Chief," Black said in his ponderous manner.

"It seems just like yesterday that I was in here," I said, taking a seat.

"You already know why you're here, Chief, so we'll proceed." He turned on his tape recorder.

I took a small digital recorder from my pocket, turned it on and set it on White's desk. "You haven't read me my warning, yet. Either Mirandize me or read the Garrity rule."

Everyone knows that the Miranda warning is to protect the Fifth Amendment right of a suspect against self-incrimination. Most people *don't* know about the Garrity ruling, which arose from a Supreme Court ruling, *Garrity versus New Jersey*, in 1967.

A police officer *can* be ordered to give evidence against himself or herself in departmental investigation that may result in firing, but such information *cannot* be used in a criminal proceeding. Once Mirandized, however, a cop becomes like any other citizen with no obligation to give evidence against himself and the right to call a lawyer.

"This is just an inquiry into a shooting," Black said.

"Nonetheless, give me the Garrity rule and I'll talk or give me the Miranda warning and I'll call my attorney."

"All right, Chief," Black said in apparent disgust. "I am now advising you under *Garrity versus New Jersey*, that a refusal to answer questions may lead to disciplinary action, including suspension or termination, but your answers cannot be used in criminal proceedings."

"All right, what do you want to know?"

"Is this your use of force statement and firearms usage report and is it true to the best of your knowledge?" He handed it to me and I examined it and handed it back.

"Yes, I wrote it and to the best of my knowledge it is correct."

"Explain why you were at the Mexicali Cantina the day you were involved in a shooting with Jorge Chávez," White chimed in.

"I was attempting to serve a subpoena on Chávez."

"As chief of detectives, is it part of your normal duties to deliver subpoenas?" Black asked, with what appeared to be a slight glint of smugness in his eyes.

"As a matter of fact, serving court documents is the basic duty of *all* sheriff's deputies. In addition, I deliver them by the dozens to the officers working for me. To elaborate, though, I don't have to, my companion, who is an attorney, asked me to serve that particular subpoena. As you may recall, it's a common practice and was in the long ago days when you two were *real* cops."

"You will agree, though, Chief Tempest, that no shooting would have occurred had you not been doing a favor for a private attorney?" Black's face had flushed at my mention of *real* cops.

"True, and if the Earth hadn't been hit by a large comet, there would probably still be a lot of dinosaurs around."

"Chief Tempest," the tall, lean White said, "you shot Chávez with a nine millimeter Glock. Are you aware that .40 caliber is standard departmental issue?"

"I am aware of that. Are you aware that the Glock nine millimeter is the pistol with which I qualified at the range, and that I haven't been issued a Glock .40 caliber?"

White ignored my question. "Did you identify yourself as a police officer to Jorge Chávez, Chief Tempest."

"Yes, I did."

"Did you display your badge and ID?" Black asked.

"No I didn't. There wasn't time."

"So for all Jorge Chávez knew you could have been an armed robber when you entered the kitchen with a weapon in your hand?" Black continued.

"I had no weapon in my hand when I entered that kitchen. I did not draw my weapon until the suspect had already fired the first round at me."

"At exactly which point did you identify yourself as a police officer?" White asked.

"Between the time he bolted out the back door and the time he fired the first round. As you know, things get murky during a gunfight. Well, maybe *you* don't know."

White flushed and it was prominent against his fish belly white complexion, but he plowed on. "One of your rounds struck Chávez in the right arm — is that what you were aiming for?"

"No, I aimed for center of mass just like I had been trained."

"What was your backdrop?" Black asked.

"The hundred foot, kudzu-covered embankment behind him. The one from which you recovered the other two rounds."

"Chief, how many shootings have you been involved in?" White asked.

"Three. One in 1985, one five weeks ago, and the one yesterday."

"So, you had to fire a weapon once in your first fifteen years, and now you've been involved in two shootings in the last two months. Do you think it could be a difference in judgment because of your health problems?"

"Now you're speculating and asking me to speculate. This interview's over. I have police work to do."

"It's over when *we* say it's over," Black said.
"Good day, *gentlemen*." I picked up my recorder and left.

Five

The University of Tennessee was founded in 1794 in Knoxville as Blount College. The campus sprawls across what would be called small mountains anywhere but East Tennessee, west of old downtown Knoxville on the banks of the Tennessee River.

On game days, the UT campus turns into a sea of orange in support of UT athletes whose uniforms are orange and white. The population of Knox County is 400 thousand-plus and growing. The joke is that the population exceeds half a million on an important game day and it may well be true.

I was on campus, hoping to speak to Professor Tiberius Jonathon Wyatt. As I approached his office, the door was standing open. I knocked on the door frame and he looked up from behind his desk. It was obvious from his expression that he wasn't pleased to see me.

"Come in," he said. The odor of pipe tobacco told me I had been right about his smoking habits.

"You may remember me, Professor. I'm Shy Tempest, Chief of Detectives from the sheriff's office."

"Yes, I remember you. I've already been interviewed by detectives from the Knoxville Police Department. I don't think I have to speak with you."

"Under the United States Constitution, Professor, you didn't *have* to speak to them. But most people have no problem with helping the police to solve crimes — especially murder."

"Oh, all right. Come in and sit down, but I can't talk long."

"Thank you." I took a seat across from his desk and from my vantage point, I could see several weapons displayed in a glass case behind his desk.

"I understand your specialty is ancient civilizations?"

"Actually, to be more specific, Chief Tempest, my field of specialty is Mesoamerican cultures." He turned his stylishly trimmed Vandyke in my direction with barely concealed contempt.

"Such as the Aztecs," I said.

"Among many others, including the Maya, Mixtecs, Incas and Zapotecs. Amateurs tend to see things in a rather limited way."

"I was admiring your collection of weapons. The bigger one is a *macuahuitl,* isn't it, the Aztec version of a sword with obsidian embedded in the edges? I see you have an *atlatl*, a dart or spear thrower as well as some nice obsidian knives."

"Very good, Mister Tempest. Are you a student of anthropology or ancient warfare?"

"No, I just read a lot. In fact, I've read your book, *The Puzzles of Mesoamerica.*"

"I hope you didn't read it just to curry favor with me. It wasn't exactly a New York bestseller like two of your novels."

"No, I read it several years ago while doing research for a magazine article."

He seemed in a much better humor. "Well then, Mister Tempest, I'm impressed. Of course, I'm sure you do your job well enough to know that I had a run-in with the law a while back. Are you interested in what happened?"

I shrugged. "I noticed there was no disposition, so I assumed the charge was bogus."

"Do you mind if I light up my pipe?" He took it from his pocket and knocked the wattle into a large ceramic ashtray. "If you're a smoker, feel free to light up. I'm a bit politically incorrect on the matter."

As he went through the pipe-smokers ritual, I lit up a filtered Camel. "Are you originally from the United Kingdom, Professor?"

"Heaven's no, I'm from a little town in Kentucky. I suppose I picked up a bit of an accent when I was studying at Oxford."

I had him eating out of my hand after that.

"Are any of those weapons original?" I asked.

"No, they're replicas. At one time they were hard to find, but as Marshall McLuhan predicted, the world is turning into a global village, especially with the Internet. Now most things can be had from almost anywhere."

"Yes, a very interesting book, *The Medium is the Massage*. The one McLuhan did with Quentin Fiore."

"You continue to amaze me, Mister Tempest. Where did you attend university?"

"I never did. As I said, I just read a lot.

"Even more remarkable, then. Did you want to hear about my brush with the law? The Knoxville police detectives did."

"If you wish, Professor. Please call me Shy."

"Very well, Shy. And please call me Jon. Have you ever fenced, Shy?"

"No, I never have, Jon."

"Well, the laughable story about my short incarceration arose from a fencing match, too much wine and the presence of some young women."

"*Cherche la femme*," I said.

"How true that is. Anyway, Donald Crawford, a friend of mine who teaches English literature, and I were at a party. Our host had a set of foils displayed that were *not* for fencing. Both of us had fenced in college, so we took them down, showing off a bit, I suppose, and one thing led to another. He got the worst of it and filed charges against me. Once he calmed down, we worked it out. A bit boring, eh?"

"No I find it quite interesting," I said. "You say it isn't difficult to order these Aztec replica weapons?"

"Well, anyone who can afford it, could easily have one. I'll give you the name of the supplier where I got mine," he said.

"Professor, what I'm about to tell you must remain in strict confidence."

"Of course," he said, leaning forward. If you want a friend for life, tell him a secret.

"Jerry Carpenter may have very well been attacked by something similar to a *macuahuitl.* Do you know anyone else who might collect such weapons?"

"Really, a *macuahuitl?* That would be one for the books, wouldn't it? It just so happens I *do* know somebody who has a large collection of ancient replica weapons. His name is Jed Osteen. A very unstable lad who often shows up for our informal study group. Very argumentative boy."

"I would certainly be interested in sitting in on that study group, Jon."

"Well, you have the luck of the Irish with you. We're meeting in half an hour at my house. You're welcome to sit in."

"That *is* luck," I said, feigning surprise. I had led him right where I intended him to go. "I have my car with me; I could follow you."

Half an hour later, I was at Jon Wyatt's home in an area called Holston Hills. His house was very nice, but over fifty years old. It was an area that had started out upper middle class and stayed around long enough to become quaint. The houses in the area had mostly been kept up well by their owners, first and second generations.

"I love this hardwood, Jon. You hardly ever see it these days," I told him as he set out a bowl of punch along with nuts, cookies and chips.

"It was pretty shoddy when I bought it," he said, "but I've put a lot of work into it. By the way, that stack of pictures on the end of the table is of one of our discussion group meetings. Take a look if you like, while I take care of a few details in the kitchen."

I picked up the pictures and thumbed through them. There was a picture of Jerry Carpenter, Professor Wyatt and three younger men, all holding glasses or clear plastic cups, in the awkward stance that men take when being photographed. I noticed that there were two copies of every picture, so I slipped a copy of the five men into my pocket.

"There's the doorbell. Have a seat, Shiloh and let me welcome the rest of my guests," Wyatt said, hurrying back through the dining room.

The first cluster of four women, included Deborah Clark, who raised her eyebrows but made no inquiry as to why I was there. Within ten minutes everyone was there. There were ten women and four men, counting Jon Wyatt. We all gathered in his large living room and found seats.

"We have a special guest tonight," Wyatt said. "Chief of Detectives Shy Tempest, who in addition to being a pretty famous police officer has also had two novels on the New York Times bestseller list. He went around the room, introducing them. I smiled and nodded at everyone, but I was focused on the three male students, Jed Osteen, Ronald Oxendine and Mike Weaver.

"Who wants to open the discussion tonight, and on what particular subject?" Wyatt asked.

"Let's talk about Jerry Carpenter's murder," Jed Osteen said. "That's why the cop is here, right?" Osteen was dark in complexion, short black hair, a medium but husky build and dark eyes with an unnatural brightness.

"Jed!" Deborah Carpenter spoke sharply. "Chief Tempest was a close personal friend of Jerry's. The Knoxville city police are investigating, not the department for which Shiloh works. If you want to stay tonight, act civilized."

"Nobody's talking about it," Osteen continued, "but it's obvious to me what happened to Jerry Carpenter. He was sacrificed to *Huitzilopochtli*, the Aztec god of the sun and war! Who wants to bet that the police found Jerry with his heart ripped out and burned at the scene?"

As Osteen spoke, I saw Professor Wyatt go pale, but he recovered quickly. "That is utterly ridiculous and simplistic!"

Osteen colored slightly and snapped back. "When the sunlight hits the Sunsphere at sundown or at daybreak, it could *be* the sun."

Despite all my years as a cop and poker player, it was difficult to remain stoic. He had described Jerry's murder — and suddenly the bits of charcoal found at the scene made sense. There had probably been a portable charcoal grill but the killer had been frightened away by something or someone."

"Mister Osteen, apparently your imagination is getting the better of you," Wyatt said.

"Or he's off his meds again," the young man who had been introduced as Ronald Oxendine said laconically. Oxendine was also darkly complected with short, dark hair, which we had called a "burr" when I was a kid. The short, short haircuts are as popular now as the Beatle cuts had been in my young adult life.

"I don't need medications!" Osteen turned towards Oxendine and almost growled the words. Apparently, their feud was of long-standing.

"You *need* them, you just don't take them," Oxendine said.

"All right," Wyatt broke in. "Time out. Let's get some refreshments and chill a little."

"I'll chill somewhere else, if you don't mind!" Osteen stood abruptly and stalked out of the house. A minute or so later, I heard a motorcycle start up outside, a Japanese bike, not a Harley-Davidson.

"Shy," John Wyatt said, "I hope you'll forgive Jed. He leaves fairly often in a rage. Not the most stable person in the world. And, Ronald, it doesn't help when you engage in primate posturing with him."

"Sorry, Professor, but he annoys me sometimes," Oxendine said.

The group wandered to the table for punch and snacks. One of the female students — a brunette with a name like Buffy or Tiffany — came by and gushed about how much she loved my books and how she would like to know me better. But I don't get into women who are looking for father figures to date. I was pleasant but got away as quickly as possible.

Ronald Oxendine was standing alone at the end of the table, nibbling a handful of peanuts. I walked over and spoke. "Oxendine is a Lumbee Indian name isn't it?"

"So I've been told," he said. "It's my mother's maiden name. My father abandoned her before I was born."

"The Lumbees were a group like the Melungeons in Tennessee, the Carmelites in Virginia and the Brass Ankles and Redbones in South Carolina and Louisiana. A mixed blood group, probably with Mediterranean ancestry, shunned by white society. My grandmother was Melungeon."

"Like I said, I don't know much about it. My mother left me when I was nine and too old to be cute. I was raised in an orphanage until I was old enough to join the Army. I spent eight years as a soldier and now I'm going to school with my GI benefits."

"Jed Osteen seems to be a little odd," I said.

"A *little* odd? He's around the bend crazy! His parents are wealthy and pay for his college, when he takes the trouble to show up. Most of the time he spends writing about his warrior fantasies. He has a collection of ancient weapons you wouldn't believe."

"You've seen them?" I said.

"Jed talked several members of the study group into going to his house before we knew how nuts he was. He once got arrested, you know, running naked in the civic coliseum. Well, he was carrying a Roman short sword and wearing a metal helmet."

"Sounds very disturbed," I said.

"He's obsessed with death, dying and killing. I'm surprised he hasn't been locked up in a looney bin," Oxendine said.

Wyatt called the group back together and some one brought up the subject of theology among primitive people. I followed most of the discussion, marveling at how silly they sounded. I had been carrying a rifle for Uncle Sam when I was younger than most of them.

Mike Weaver, the third male student, was a pale youngster with wispy, almost white hair. He apparently suffered from some kind of neurological disorder. Even lifting a plate caused tremors in his arm. I decided he could be dismissed as a suspect.

The group began to break up with the exit of two of the female students. Once the exodus started, Deborah Clark, Jon

Wyatt and I were quickly alone. We began to carry glasses and dishes to the kitchen to load in the dishwasher.

"Jon, what did you think of Jed Osteen's theory?" I asked.

"It's a typical adolescent idea of what life was like among the Aztecs. It wasn't just humans they sacrificed. There were also animals, produce, gold utensils and even dirt offered to *Huitzilopochtli* and other gods. Aztec theology was complicated."

"It seems I've read about warriors with their hearts torn out and burned on Aztec altars," I said. "But you're the expert, Jon." I said.

"No, you have read it because it happened. I just feel compelled to point out that identifying one particular type of sacrifice as representative of the Aztec pantheon of gods and worship is like viewing Palm Sunday as representative of Christianity. It's simplistic."

"So the ritual Osteen described *was* an Aztec rite?"

"Yes, on occasion it was. It wasn't an everyday event."

"In *Cannibals and Kings*, Marvin Harris said a shortage of protein was behind some cannibalism in Mesoamerica. Is that true?"

"It's a theory," Wyatt said. "Not everybody agrees."

"Well, Shiloh, how did you like our little group?" Deborah Clark asked.

"Interesting, but I don't have the patience to deal with the excesses of idealism most students exhibit. I guess I'm old and cynical. Jon, I hope I'll be able to call on you for help from time to time."

"By all means, Shiloh. Today has been an eye-opener. I've always found police officers to be a dull lot. Now I know it was a generalization. You can hold your own in *any* company."

"I'll take that as high praise, Jon. On that note, I think I'll head home." I said.

"Why don't you walk me to the car, Shiloh. I need to be leaving myself," Deborah Clark said. I saw a small cloud pass over Wyatt's face when she spoke.

"All right, Deborah. Jon, thanks for inviting me," I said.

Deborah picked up her purse and kissed Wyatt on the cheek. "See you at school, Jon."

"Both of you drive carefully," Wyatt said.

Outside, Deborah paused by her Volkswagen bug. It was a late model in a feminine-looking pinkish color, not one of the original workhorses. "You remind me a lot of Jerry," she said. You two were made from the same stuff."

"How's that, Deborah? We didn't have a lot in common except the old days."

"Maybe it's because you were both the type of man who make a woman feel *safe*. In my business, I come in contact with men who have very seldom lived in the real world. I feel safer alone than with most men I work with."

I saw where it was going, but waited too long to react. Suddenly, her face was close to mine and she was looking into my eyes. She was wearing some sort of musk-based perfume. She took half a step and our bodies were touching lightly. "Shy, I think I could sleep well in your arms tonight. Do you think I'm a terrible person?"

"No, Deborah," I answered, stepping back. "I think you're grieving and vulnerable and I *know* that I am in a committed relationship, but you *still* tempt me. We'd best resume this conversation another time."

"Of course," she smiled, seemingly happy that I thought she was attractive. When she turned to unlock her car, I saw Jon Wyatt looking from the picture window. I was glad looks couldn't kill and that he was not facing me or worse, behind me, with a weapon in hand.

He had seen everything and his face was a mask of rage. That I had declined probably only made it worse.

Six

Jennifer came into the kitchen, rubbing her eyes. She was wearing a dark green robe trimmed in white. Even with her mane of anthracite colored hair in disarray, sleep in her eyes and with mascara smeared, she looked better than most women. Jennifer Mendoza is a knockout in any league.

When I first saw Jennifer, she reminded me of Madeline Stowe in a movie called *Stakeout.* She was a twenty-year-old undergraduate at the University of Tennessee and I was a thirty-eight-year-old sergeant with the sheriff's office.

We were both coming out of a bad relationship. My wife had moved on to greener pastures and Jen's husband had nearly broken her spirit with beatings and abuse.

"Something smells good," she said, sitting down at the kitchen table.

I poured her a cup of coffee, black and handed it to her. "I'm whipping up a couple of omelets. Mine will have cheese, bell peppers, sausage and scallions. What's *your* pleasure?"

"Same for me. I'd keep you around for breakfast alone, even if you didn't turn out superb dinners.

"You're right. I should have been a chef instead of dodging bullets."

"Speaking of dodging bullets, you had a close call last night," Jennifer said.

"How would you know? You were asleep when I got home," I answered, sliding her omelet on a plate and putting it in front of her.

"I mean a close call with a woman wearing musky perfume. I smelled it on you when you blundered into the bedroom trying not to wake me," she said, with a bite of omelet almost to her mouth.

"How do you know it was just a *close* call?" I asked, pouring the rest of the egg mixture into the skillet.

"It wasn't *that* strong," she said. "Besides, you don't like blondes and she smelled like a blonde. Yummy. This omelet is good."

"Her name is Deborah Clark. She was Jerry Carpenter's special friend. She's the reason he was auditing a university course and going to the Thursday night study group. I decided to sit in last night."

"So, was she a blonde?"

"Yes, she was, and a cheerleader in high school," I said, folding my omelet.

"Now I *know* she's not your type. One cheerleader in a lifetime is enough for any man and you already had one," Jennifer said.

I slid my omelet on to a plate, got Tobasco and doused my creation with hot sauce. I sat down, picked up a piece of buttered toast from the bread dish, and got a fork full of omelet. Jennifer was right. The omelet was good.

"Is Jorge Chávez going to testify for your client," I asked taking a sip of coffee from my favorite mug, a one of a kind with a pig on it. A friend had made it for me.

"Better than that. Jorge produced a respectable Anglo businessman to testify that he and my client were working in his warehouse the night of the alleged rape," she said.

"How did you pull that off?"

"I promised Jorge I'd represent him for shooting at you." She took a bite of omelet and chewed slowly.

I put down my coffee cup and looked at her to see if she was kidding. I saw that she wasn't. She picked up a piece of toast and began to spread apple butter on it.

"Jennifer, your client tried to kill me!"

"It was a misunderstanding, Shiloh. He thought you were

from immigration. Besides, he didn't actually *shoot* you. In fact, you shot him."

"Shooting at immigration officers is also illegal, Jennifer. What defense do you intend to offer — that I was armed and dangerous?"

"I hadn't thought about that one," she said, taking a bite of toast.

"You can't do this, Jen. Get someone else from your firm to handle it. It's a conflict of interest."

"Not for me. I'm grateful he wasn't a better shot."

"We'll discuss this later. I have to get ready for work," I said.

"Does this mean you're not agreeable to letting him plead to a lesser charge at this time?"

I didn't answer her.

I called Tom Abernathy and Rex Claiborne to meet me at a little restaurant named Rankin on Central Avenue. I had decided not to put them on a spot by showing up at the Knoxville Police Department.

My coffee had just arrived when they walked in. "What's up, Officers?"

"We're hoping you can tell us," Abernathy said, sliding into the booth across from me. Claiborne sat beside him, remaining as silent as Harpo Marx without his horn.

"I had an interesting afternoon and evening yesterday..." I stopped talking as the waitress brought two more cups and a pot of coffee. She put the cups on the table, poured the coffee and left. She was apparently used to cops.

"So tell us about it," Abernathy said.

I took a sip of coffee. "I talked to Professor Wyatt and went to the Thursday evening study group."

"How did you manage that?" Abernathy asked. "He acted like we were something stuck to his shoes."

"I blew a little smoke up his ass, mentioned I had read his book and admired his collection of ancient Aztec weapons."

"The things in the case behind his desk?" Abernathy asked.

"The very same. Did you notice the thing that looked like a cross between a sword and a club. It's called a *macuahuitl,* and it may have been the type of weapon used to bash Jerry in the back of the head. The *macuahuitl* is made of wood and has obsidian embedded in the edges to make it sharp."

"You mean those things behind him were *real*?"

"No, they're replicas, but Jed Osteen has a huge selection of ancient weapons, including a *macuahuitl.* Members of the class have seen the collection."

"Those things were no match for steel," Claiborne, said, contempt in his voice. "A few conquistadors beat the entire Aztec army."

"That's true, Rex. But the *macuahuitl* was good for disabling enemy warriors. Bringing a prisoner back carried more prestige than killing him."

"Who told you about this weapon collection?" Abernathy asked.

"An older student, a military veteran, named Ronald Oxendine."

"We interviewed him and he didn't mention the weapons to us," Abernathy said.

I shrugged. "That wasn't what I needed to tell you anyway. Last night, Jed Osteen speculated as to how and why Jerry was murdered. He said Jerry was sacrificed to the Aztec sun and war god, then described Jerry's disembowelment and said Jerry's heart had probably been burned at the site. That explains the charcoal."

"How did he know those things unless he was there?" Claiborne asked.

"Osteen *may* have been there, but the ceremony is in history books. Captive warriors would be sacrificed by the Aztecs on a stone altar and their hearts would be ripped out while they were still beating, then burned," I said.

"So, the Sunsphere represents the sun god?" Abernathy said.

"That's Osteen's theory and it's the most plausible I've heard so far."

"It would have been nice if you had held Osteen for us," Claiborne said.

"On what grounds? There are no warrants outstanding for him and I don't have jurisdiction. Besides, I didn't want to spook him and make him start dodging you two."

"If Osteen killed Jerry, do you think he's dumb enough to have kept the... what did you call it?"

"It's a *macuahuit.* Other Mesoamerican people called it a *macana*. That word, *macana,* has a broader meaning these days — it can even refer to a police nightstick. *Macuahuitl* was the Aztec word, though."

"But do you think he's dumb enough to have held on to it?" Abernathy repeated the question.

"Tom, from what I saw last night, Osteen may be too mentally ill to appreciate the difference between reality and fantasy."

Abernathy looked thoughtful. "We don't have probable cause for a search warrant on Osteen's house. But he has a Jeep with an expired tag parked in front. I'm pretty sure there's still a city ordinance against abandoning a vehicle without a tag. *And* there's a difference between an inventory and a search, but the end result is the same."

"It's worked for me a lot of times," I said.

"Well, that was what I had on your case. I'm sure you'll use the information wisely. I need to go by my own office and check in."

"Hey, Chief," Abernathy said as I stood up."

"Yes?"

"Had you really read his book?"

"Of course. Coffee's on me," I said on the way out. Restaurants seldom charge cops for coffee.

"It's nice to see we still got a chief of detectives," Al Reagan said, in a voice more a growl than human speech. I looked up and he was standing in my office doorway with John Freed. The red-headed Freed is as thin as Reagan is broad.

A more dissimilar pair would have been hard to find. In his early forties, Reagan has dark, thinning hair cut to the scalp. Freed, in his late twenties, has wavy carrot top hair.

"Yeah Chief. Where you been keeping yourself?" Freed asked in a tremulous, almost contralto voice.

"Reagan," I said, "I still have my request to the Sheriff for a new lieutenant on my desk." If you think I'm falling behind, I can have you temporarily promoted to take up the slack."

"You don't have to threaten me, Chief. I do enough paper-work now."

"Hey, Chief, how come you never threaten to promote me?" Freed asked.

"I don't want to ruin what's left of your youth, John. Al's already over the hill."

"He's in a hateful mood today," Reagan said. "I guess he ain't interested in taking us out to eat at the Regas now that he's a chief."

"Who's going to the Regas?" Sheriff Sam Renfro asked, sticking his head in the squad room. "Which officer under my command can afford to eat at Regas?"

"We thought *you* might spring for it and write it off as a business expense, Sam," I said.

"Well, hell then. Let's *go*," he said. Meet me in the sally-port garage."

He was gone without further conversation. Sam's always been that way.

"Was he serious?" Freed asked.

"Sam never kids about food," I said. "You heard the man. Let's go meet him in the sally-port."

Twenty minutes later we were standing in the lobby at the Regas. It has been said by some that ninety percent of the big business deals in Knoxville are closed at the Regas. On any given day, high-ranking politicians and captains of industry can be seen coming and going around lunch time.

There are higher priced restaurants these days, but the Regas is still the flagship of commerce and politics and famous for its red velvet cake.

Several people hailed the sheriff as we were escorted to a highly visible table and he made small talk with each of them briefly. When we were seated, Sam said in a low voice, "This is the pain in the ass part of being sheriff. *Everybody* sucks up."

A waitress came to the table and asked what we wanted to drink. "Four coffees," Sam said.

"*Three* coffees and a diet Sprite," I corrected him.

Sam looked at me, and feigned surprise. "You're drinking *Sprite?*"

"No, but Freed does and I knew *he* wasn't going to correct you."

"You don't drink coffee, Freed? And I'd heard such good things about you."

"Well, uh, caffeine disagrees with me, Sheriff," Freed almost stammered.

"All right, that makes sense," Sam said. "But you order some sissy dessert like Crème Brûlée and you're out of here."

"I never had that before, Sheriff." Freed was not sure if Sam was kidding.

"How are things in criminal investigation, Reagan?" Sam asked.

"Good, Sheriff. We have a chief we can work with *and* a sheriff that let's us do our jobs," the big detective said.

"You're not blowing smoke, are you Reagan?" Sam asked.

"Nope, that's not my style, Sheriff."

"I've been trying to get Reagan to bid on the lieutenant's job, Sam, but he doesn't think he'd like the paperwork," I said.

"A good street cop never does, but somebody has to be in charge. You might want to think about it, Reagan. I have a lot of faith in Shy's judgment — most of the time.

"How's the KPD investigation on Jerry Carpenter's murder going?" Sam asked, changing the subject.

"They're working some good leads. I'm helping when they ask for it. So far they've kept me updated."

"I heard somebody cut Carpenter's heart out. Is that true, Shy?" Reagan asked.

I smiled and shook my head and smiled. "Two men can keep a secret if one of them's dead. Yeah, it's supposed to be under wraps, but it's true."

"His heart was cut out? Gee whizz," Freed said.

"Freed, do you even know *how* to swear?" Sam asked. "I've heard you don't"

"Well, yeah. I know *how*. I just don't do it except when I'm really upset."

"Al, I told Jennifer I'd be home early today, would you do a little research for me?"

"Sure" He got out his police officer's constant companion notebook and a pen.

"The name is Carol Oxendine. She's a white female and should be in her mid-forties if she's still around. Dig up whatever you can find. I'll get it in the morning."

At that point the waitress came back with our drinks and to take our orders. We all became focused on the food.

Seven

"Wake up, Sleepyhead. I have your morning coffee." I opened my eyes and Jennifer was standing by the bed, holding a cup of coffee with a wet towel around her head, wearing nothing else. It was a pleasant way to be awakened.

"To what do I owe this pleasure, and is this an invitation?"

"*Hombres* are all alike. You wake up to find a naked woman standing by the bed with a cup of coffee and you think she's a *puta.*" She put the coffee down and kissed me, but darted away as I reached for her instead of the coffee.

"Look but don't touch. I have an early deposition. What to wear? What to wear?" She stood in front of the closet and stared.

"Did I ever tell you how much you resemble Madeline Stowe when she played in *The Stakeout*?"

"Only about a thousand times," she took out a blue skirt and a pale blue blouse. "Do these match."

"You're asking a man who wears plaid shirts for fashion advice? I was about to tell you that it was the same view of Madeline Stowe as I have of you right now that made me lust after her in the shower scene."

"You really need to get over that, Shiloh. I'm sure I look better than Madeline Stowe these days. That film was made twenty years ago." Jennifer said, stepping into lacy blue panties.

"Are you still upset that I'm going to represent Jorge Chávez? You were grumpy all evening." She fastened a matching blue bra in the back.

"Are you still going to represent him?"

"Yes." She pulled up and buttoned the skirt and reached for the blouse.

"Then I'm still upset."

"But I brought you coffee, *Shiloh,*" and strutted around naked." She buttoned the blouse and tucked it into her skirt. "That should count for *something.*"

"You've *always* been a lady in public and a *puta* in bed — but the fact remains, your new client tried to shoot me!"

"Well, everyone is entitled to a good defense. This is the United States." She took the towel from around her head, shook it out and picked up her hair dryer.

"You have an entire firm of lawyers around you who *don't* cohabit with the man your client tried to kill, Jen." She turned on the dryer and her hair fanned out around her head.

"But no one owes Jorge a favor. He's going to keep an innocent man from going to prison for rape. Besides, I have letters from three employers attesting to Jorge's good character and work ethic."

"He *still* tried to shoot me! Jorge Chávez placed my life in jeopardy as well as the lives of people driving by. Not to mention that he caused me to do a ton of paperwork and be interviewed by IAD."

"We all make mistakes, Shiloh." She turned off the dryer and ran a comb through her still damp hair. It was all she needed to face the world. My Latina beauty wears little makeup and doesn't need it.

"We'll talk about it again later. I have to go to this deposition." She leaned over and kissed me, leaving the smell of orange blossoms.

"Nothing will change," I said as she went out the door. "He tried to shoot me."

A moment later, I heard the garage door opening and then her car started.

It was a pleasant morning, so I took the scenic route to work. As I sat at the intersection of Central Avenue Pike and Callahan, dispatch put out a call to patrol that a man was trying to kill a dog with a baseball bat at a subdivision a short distance away.

"Unit 4, I'm at Central and Callahan, I'll be responding to the animal cruelty call."

"Ten-4, you're the closest unit, Chief."

I turned into the subdivision and hit the accelerator. Neighbors were outside, watching as a man with a full-sized bat, drunkenly staggered after a predominantly black German Shepherd. The shepherd was limping as she ran along the inside of the chainlink fence.

Stopping abruptly. I got out of my cruiser, picking up a collapsible police baton that was seven inches closed, but expanded to sixteen inches. I went through the gate and held up my badge case with the seven-pointed star. "Police! Back away from that dog."

The man stopped, turned slowly in the manner of drunks and looked at me. He was six-feet, maybe two-forty, his head was shaved. He had a tiger's head tattooed on one forearm and a dragon on the other. "I'm in my own yard and this is *my* dog. She growled and bared her teeth at me."

"You're drunk in a public place and you're committing a felony. Drop the ball bat and come over here."

"I'm comin' over there all right — to throw you out of my yard, *old man*. I don't care what kind of cop you are."

He advanced on me unsteadily and I prepared myself for what I expected. He got within four feet of me and swung the ball bat. Just before he went into his swing, I snapped the collapsible baton downward, stepped inside the arc of the bat and drove the baton into his solar plexus. He deflated like a balloon against a cactus and I rolled him over and put my handcuffs on him as he was trying to get his breath back.

The German Shepherd, was standing about twenty feet away, watching. I dropped to one knee and said, "Come here girl, come here."

After a moment's hesitation she ran to me, limping and pushed her snout under my arm. Her body was trembling. One of the women spectators called out. "Her name is Magdala."

"It's going to be okay, Magdala." She flinched as a police cruiser screeched to a halt and a young patrol officer jumped from his cruiser and ran to us.

He stopped and smiled. "Guess you didn't need any help, huh, Chief?"

"Yes, I do. I don't have a cage in my car. Take this whining punk to jail and tell them to hold him until the *old man* who kicked his ass gets there to book him.

"The charges will be, aggravated assault against a police officer and aggravated animal cruelty. If you will, get the names of the witnesses before you transport him. I'm going to take Magdala and have her checked for injuries."

The young officer looked puzzled until I clarified my statement. "Magdala is the German Shepherd who *used* to belong to the suspect."

I stood and said, "Come along Magdala." She followed me out of the yard, still limping a little, and when I opened my cruiser door, she jumped right in the back. Suddenly I heard clapping. I turned and saw that the patrol officer was putting the big man into his cruiser. His neighbors were giving him a send-off.

A veterinarian I knew was about five minutes away. Magdala lay quietly in the back seat and I could see that she had quit trembling.

When we entered the front door of the animal hospital, Lola Parker, the veterinarian was standing at the front desk looking at a chart. A fortyish woman, dressed in khaki shorts and hiking boots, she spoke. "What do we have here, Shy? Why is Magdala limping?"

"I just caught her owner trying to kill her with a baseball bat. How do you know her name?"

"I know her owner. I gave her all her inoculations. And Roy Jamison, her owner is a jerk. Take her to the exam room," Lola said.

"Come on, girl." Magdala followed me into the exam room

and sat down. Lola came in and dropped to one knee to examine her.

After running her hands all over Magdala's body, Lola lifted the injured leg and worked the joints gently. "Shy, she has no broken bones I can see. No damage to the head. But in light of the fact that he was hitting her with a blunt object, I'd like to watch her for a few hours."

"All right." Before I could say anything else, my cell phone rang. "Hello, Chief Tempest here." I listened quietly for a moment. "All right, Abernathy, I'm on my way."

"When should I pick her up, Lola?"

"We close at seven. Any time before that."

As I stood to leave, Magdala tried to follow me. I dropped to one knee and she put her snout under my arm again. "It's all right, Magdala. I'll be back after a while to get you."

She raised her head and looked me in the eyes as if deciding something. Then she relaxed and sat.

"Shy, you have just made the most loyal friend you'll ever have in your life," Lola said. "Magdala will be waiting when you come back — for the rest of her life."

When I arrived at the address Abernathy had given me, there were three KPD cruisers in front of the house. Jed Osteen was sitting in the back of one of the cruisers. I glanced at him as I walked by on my way to where Abernathy was standing.

"What's he wearing, Abernathy?"

"I'm not sure what you would call that garment. But he's dressed as a Roman soldier. There's the helmet he was wearing by the front porch. And there's his short sword a few feet to the left where he fell when he was hit by the Taser," Abernathy said.

"This morning, there was a message on my desk that said, 'The murder weapon is in Jed Osteen's house.' I checked the tape that came in through teleserve, non-emergency and it sounded as if the caller was using a cheap voice synthesizer, the kind that comes with Halloween costumes.

"The magistrate said we still didn't have enough for a search warrant, so we decided to pull the Jeep with the expired tag as an abandoned vehicle and see if we could draw Osteen out.

"We drew him out all right. He charged out on the porch wearing a steel helmet and waving a sword around. When he came off the porch, one of the patrol officers tazed him.

"Rex is picking up the search warrant now and I thought you might want to be here when we executed it."

"An anonymous tip, huh?" I said. "How convenient."

"Yep. Apparently somebody who didn't know much about how the law works," Abernathy replied.

"What kind of alibi did Jon Wyatt have for the night Jerry was killed?"

"Not a good one. Home alone, grading papers and watching television. Is there something I need to know?"

"The night I went to the study group at Wyatt's house, as Deborah Clark and I were leaving, she came on to me pretty hard. Wyatt was watching out the window but didn't know I saw him. His expression was murderous. He's got it bad for her."

"Chief Tempest, you were going to tell me this, *when*?"

"You were already looking at him. To tell the truth, this was a sort of Southern gentleman thing, Abernathy. I've always despised men who boast about sexual conquests."

"Yeah, they both admitted a past relationship, but neither of them indicated it was anything but casual," Abernathy said.

"As far as Deborah Clark is concerned, it never was anything but casual. I'm sure Wyatt wants more. It must have really galled him to see Deborah leaving with an old cop like Jerry. Maybe he even sensed how serious it was."

"I suppose I'll have to look at him a lot harder, now. Rex is back with the search warrant, let's take a look inside," Abernathy said.

The door was still open, so we just walked in, pulling on latex gloves. We were followed in by a team of forensic technicians.

"Holy crap," Rex Claiborne said. "There must be a fortune in weapons here. I haven't seen so many swords, spears and knives since I saw Russell Crowe in *Gladiator*. When did Osteen ever have time to go to school?"

Claiborne was right. Every type of bladed weapon I had ever seen was displayed on the walls, laying on tables or standing in a corner. Everything from *machuahuitls* to fantasy blades that had never existed except in imagination, including what I recognized as a Klingon weapon from the *Star Trek* series.

"Fan out," Abernathy told the technicians. We're looking for something that may resemble one of *these*. He pointed to the *machuahuitls*. If what we're looking for is here, it may be out of sight. There may also be a knife made of obsidian. Be careful. I understand the blades can be sharper than razors."

"In addition to his other problems, Osteen apparently has an obsessive compulsive disorder, Abernathy. Except for the clutter of weapons, this place is spotless and neat. All his books are on the shelf neatly, there's no dust on anything." I noted.

"Maybe he has a maid service," Claiborne said.

We walked into the kitchen and it was also spotless. No dishes in the sink, the trash can was empty and the black and white tiles sparkled.

"Detective Abernathy," one of the evidence techs had come to the door. "I think we've found what we were looking for."

In the bedroom, the evidence technician got down on his knees and lifted the neatly made bedspread. "One of those things you pointed out and — the one that looks like a seven or eight inch blade."

"Shoot your pictures and bring them out," Abernathy said.

I followed Abernathy and Claiborne out on the porch. "All neatly tied in a package," I said. "I'll bet a thousand dollars against a hundred that you've found what you came for."

"Let's walk out to the street and smoke," Abernathy said.

On the sidewalk, where we wouldn't contaminate the evidence, Abernathy and I lit up and took a couple of deep drags each. A few minutes later, the evidence technician came out carrying the *machuahuitl* and an obsidian knife with a leather thong wrapped around the haft, apparently for a tighter grip.

"The leather haft looks like it has been soaked in blood and there's a chip broken off one of the blades embedded in the side of this thing — whatever it was you called it."

"Bag them up," Abernathy said. Then turning to me, "I hate shooting fish in a barrel, especially when the fish don't even try to get away."

"You're right," I said. "Now that you have all this evidence, it looks like this investigation has just begun."

Magdala's ears went up when Jennifer's car pulled into the garage. I was sitting in my easy chair in the sunroom we had built onto the house a few years before, sipping a cup of Venezuelan coffee.

When Jennifer came into the living room, the German Shepherd stood and looked at her, a rumbling coming from deep in her chest. "No, Magdala, she belongs here. Come over and pet her, Jen."

As soon as I spoke, the aggression went out of the big dog. She sat and licked Jennifer's hand as Jen scratched between her ears. "You're a beauty," Jennifer said. "Shiloh has always preferred his girls a little darker than most gringos."

Jennifer kicked off her shoes and poured herself a cup of black coffee. "I saw the water bowl and food dish in the kitchen. Have you already taken Magdala shopping?" The dog's ears went up at the sound of her name.

"No, Lola Parker gave me the dog dishes, a leash and some dog food when I picked Magdala up this evening."

"How is Lola? I haven't seen her since Lilac died." Lilac was Jennifer's Miniature Schnauzer. She had lived to be nearly eighteen years old.

"Lola's the same as always." Magdala made herself comfortable by my chair again, with a sigh.

"You and Magdala made the afternoon news and the six o'clock news today. Have you seen it?" Jennifer said.

"No, the news crew must have shown up after I left this

morning. I had several messages from the news media in my box, but I didn't call them back."

"You're quite the hero," Jennifer said, "and you've brought your damsel in distress home with you. That part, I don't mind. But you're not supposed to be taking on young guys with baseball bats."

"That's probably what Sam was going to tell me. I didn't call him back either. It wasn't as heroic as it sounded. The guy was real drunk," I said.

"Shiloh, Shiloh, what are we going to do with you? You take too many risks. *But* I'm going to forgive you because I know how Magdala feels. I had my first good night's sleep in years after you took *me* home.

"When do you go to court on Magdala's abuser?"

"In the morning at nine o'clock. Lola's going to keep Magdala while I go to court and every day until she's used to being here alone."

"Have you already talked to the Attorney General about this case."

"Yes, I have."

"Magdala, welcome to our house," Jennifer said, causing the dog's ears to perk up again.

Eight

Sessions Court is the first tier in Tennessee's system of justice. It's where arraignment, probable cause and the first bail hearing is set. A sessions judge can try misdemeanors, for which the maximum time to be served is eleven months and twenty-nine days, dismiss for lack of probable cause or send a felony onto the grand jury.

The docket was crowded as I walked into Judge Peggy Frank's courtroom, where she had just sat down. Roy Jamison was sitting with other jail inmates on the second row in a striped jump suit. I knew he would be there because I had asked Judge Frank for a hundred thousand dollar bond the day before. After she heard the story, she granted it.

"First we'll hear the cases in which agreement has been reached. Attorney's, approach," Peggy said.

The assistant attorney general was a young man, probably not long out of law school. I didn't know him. He and an older, balding defense attorney I knew well approached the bench, spoke to the judge and she called Jamison's name. A jail security officer walked him to the bench in handcuffs and leg irons.

"Your honor," the defense attorney said, the attorney general and I have an agreement for your approval. Mr. Jamison agrees to plead guilty to the lesser offense of simple assault. He will surrender the dog to county custody, agrees not to own another dog, will undergo anger management and enter an alcohol treatment program, while serving a year's probation, if that's satisfactory with you."

Peggy Frank has always reminded me of a Boston Terrier. Fiftyish and gray, she looked down over her reading glasses at Roy Jamison who stood in front of her with eyes downcast.

"Look at me, Mister Jamison! Do you understand the charges and the agreement your attorney has reached with the state?"

"Yes, Your Honor," Jamison said.

"Very well, Mister Jamison. I am going to accept this plea with great reluctance because you have committed *two* heinous crimes as far as I'm concerned. I think you're a bully and a coward. You beat a helpless dog with a baseball bat and then tried to strike a police officer who is nearly sixty years old and who happens to have a bad heart...."

There was a burst of laughter from the seated officers at the side of the courtroom. The judge glared at them and they all shifted uncomfortably in their seats.

"Had he used lethal force against you, rather than simply disabling you, there would have been no questions asked. Rest assured," the judge said, "if it had been left to me, you'd sit in jail and think about what you did — not that I think you have much of a conscience.

"However, I will approve this agreement. Be certain that if you violate it in any way, I *will* have you sitting in jail. Step over there, with your attorney and sign the necessary paperwork."

As I left the courtroom, several young officers stood to shake my hand and pat me on the back. One of them whispered, "The snow on the roof doesn't mean the fire in the furnace has burned out."

As I stepped out of the back door to the court room, a hand clamped down on my shoulder. "Hang on a minute, old warrior, and I'll walk down with you."

"What brings the High Sheriff of Knox County to sessions court," I asked.

"Well, his chief of detectives didn't call him back yesterday, Shy."

"I figured you were going to chew me out for jumping a patrol call. I decided to let you cool off overnight."

"Had Jennifer cooled off by the time she saw you?" He stepped up beside me as we left the hallway and headed towards the elevators on the mezzanine.

"Yeah, did she call *you*?"

"When it broke on television, she called. That's when I left the message for you. She was fit to be tied, Shy. And I don't blame her."

"Sam, I'm like an old Beagle. The rabbit runs, I chase. I'm never going to change."

"That's what I told Jennifer. I take it you're still together this morning?"

"So far," I replied. "She likes my new dog."

"The media people want to interview you, Shy. I've called a press conference. I'd count it as a personal favor. It's good publicity and it's going to take a lot of good publicity to make up for the bad taste left by my predecessor and your predecessor, the one you killed in the squad room. Besides, Hoss, you did a good thing."

"All right, Sam. I owe you. When's the interview?"

"About ten minutes from now, in my office. I had them on alert and I called as soon as the ruling came down."

"I appreciate the advance warning, Sam."

"Shy, you know I take care of my people."

Television crews were setting up by the time we got to Sam's office. While he made small talk with members of the crews, I got a cup of coffee from his private pot and sat down in an easy chair. Chit-chat is his specialty not mine.

Three female reporters, each in different parts of the office, did their set-up shots, then the camera's were turned towards the wall on which the Knox County star was painted on a blue wall. The print media and their photographers stood to the side, watching.

"Shy, they're ready." Sam said. I reluctantly got up and took my place beside him, and the lights came on.

"Sheriff Renfro, I'm with the *Knoxville News Sentinel*, would you care to make a statement?"

"Sure. I'd just like to say that I'm proud of my old friend and colleague, Shy Tempest. I'm glad he saw fit to come out of retirement to be of service to me and Knox County. He is a brave police officer who comes down on the side of justice, no matter what the cost."

"Chief Tempest, Channel 10 News. Is it true you have a defibrillator in your heart to keep it beating?"

"Well, the defibrillator is actually just under the skin, but the wires do run into my heart," I answered.

"Channel 6 News here. Have you had any trouble with the defibrillator, Chief?"

"Let me answer that one, Shy," Sam said. "A week after Chief Tempest had it installed, he was injured in a scuffle with a suspect and one of the wires was pulled loose."

"Chief, Channel 8 News. How does your wife feel about your being back on active duty after over a decade off?"

"I don't have a wife, but my companion — or *compañera*, as they say in Spanish — is very supportive," I said. "I was a cop when she met me."

"Chief, would you care to enlarge on what *compañera* means?" the Channel 8 reporter asked. "I understand that your companion is Jennifer Mendoza, a prominent lawyer and of Spanish descent."

"There's no exact translation," I said. "But a *compañera* is more than a girlfriend, less than a wife. So far, she has been too wise to marry a scarred, old dog like me. She's quite competent to look after herself."

My last remark brought laughter from several of the female reporters.

"Chief, Channel 6 News again. "Where's Magdala, the German Shepherd you rescued yesterday?"

"Magdala is at a veterinarian's office, being watched over," I said, truthfully, though not completely.

"Chief, *Metropulse* here. Do you plan to adopt Magdala?"

"I will fill out an adoption request with the Knox County Animal Shelter. It will be up to them." Actually, Judge Frank had already signed a court order, giving Magdala to me but I would go through the process for the sake of appearances.

"The *Knoxville News Sentinel* again, Chief. Are you working on a new book at present?"

"I'm always working on a new book, but nothing will be out in the near future."

"Channel 10 News again, Chief, any chance of getting a picture of you and Magdala together today?"

"No. She had a rough day yesterday and she's still understandably upset."

"That will conclude the news conference," Sam said, sensing that I had endured for as long as it was safe to leave me in front of cameras. "We appreciate everyone who showed up today."

When they were gone, Sam sat down in his leather chair and leaned back. "That went very well, Shy. You've done good work since you got back. Let's celebrate with a Camel."

Sam had given up smoking fifteen years ago, but he always kept an ashtray and lighter for especially stressful days, most of which involved me in one way or another. I shook out a cigarette and he took it.

"It doesn't get any better than this, Hoss. Success is when you can get paid for doing something you would have done for nothing."

I had just gotten back to my office and was sorting through messages when Tom Abernathy called on my cell phone. "This is Tempest."

"Chief, this is Abernathy from KPD. We're about to interview Jed Osteen if you want to sit in."

"I figured Osteen would be in the lock-up ward at Lake Shore."

"We took him in for evaluation, but he refused to say he was a threat to anyone else in front of the doctors and he told them he was not suicidal, so they wouldn't admit him."

"What about advancing on you guys with a sword?"

"He told the doctors it was more like a stage prop than a weapon and he didn't intend to hurt anybody. Under Tennessee law, they really couldn't keep him. We checked with our law department and were told if the psychiatrists considered him to be in his right mind, we could question him."

"What about your boss, Frank Hodges?"

"He's out of town on one of his perpetual tours."

"I'll be right there," I said. "And I appreciate it."

Twenty minutes later, we entered the KPD interrogation room where Osteen sat. He looked up and said to me: "I knew you were at the class meeting checking us out."

It was hard for me to square *this* Jed Osteen with the raving lunatic from the day before or even the tense young man from the Thursday night study group.

"Jedediah Osteen, I have to read you your Miranda warning," Rex said.

"I know my rights, give me the waiver and I'll sign it."

"Osteen," Abernathy said, "you're not accused of vandalism or shoplifting. You're the chief suspect in a murder investigation."

"So I figured, Boss. The quicker I talk to you, the quicker you can clear me."

Claiborne slid a Miranda warning across the table along with a pen. Osteen glanced at it, then signed without hesitation.

"Where were you the night Jerry Carpenter was killed?" Abernathy asked.

"I was in my parent's cabin in Gatlinburg."

"Can your parents verify that?" Abernathy continued. "Or is there anyone else who can verify that you were there?"

"No, I went up there to be alone. Sometimes I don't like being around people. That's where I usually go when I want to be alone."

"Did you make any calls from Gatlinburg or log onto the Internet, anything that might have left a record we can confirm. Or did you buy anything or stop for gas." Claiborne asked.

"No, I took my motorcycle and didn't stop anywhere between."

"How well did you know Jerry Carpenter?" Abernathy asked.

"As well as you know anyone you've only been acquainted with for a couple of months." Osteen shrugged.

"Was your relationship cordial?" Claiborne asked.

"I went drinking with him at a titty bar once. And he brought his girlfriend to my house one night."

"Are you referring to Doctor Carpenter?" Abernathy inquired.

"No, but everybody in the group knew he was banging *her* on Thursdays. That Jerry was a player. But the one he brought to my place was a redheaded dancer from the titty bar. Her name was Stella, Sable or maybe Sadie. That was the night I gave Jerry a *hucahuahtl* and an obsidian knife."

"And why would you have done that, Jed?" Abernathy asked.

"Well, while me an Jerry were talking about how the Aztecs sacrificed prisoners and cut out their hearts for the Sun and War gods, I got out a *hucahuahtl* and an obsidian knife to show his girlfriend what they did it with.

"They were both impressed and I had several of each. I was in a mellow mood from smoking the pot Jerry and his girlfriend had brought, so I gave them to Jerry." Osteen said, "Besides, my parent's are rich and pay the bills as long as I stay away."

"Jed, would these be the Aztec weapons you gave Jerry?" Abernathy opened a folder and laid out two 8 x 10 glossies of the *hucahuahtl* and obsidian knife with a ruler beside each one for perspective.

"If it looks like them, it probably *is* them. You don't find them laying around in just everyone's house." Osteen said.

"Can you explain how they turned up under your bed, covered with Jerry Carpenter's blood or why a missing chip from the *hucahuahtl* was embedded in his skull?"

"No, I can't. The last time I saw those two pieces, Jerry had them. But everyone knows I hardly ever lock the doors because I'm always losing my keys."

"Somehow, we can't believe Jerry clubbed himself from behind, cut out his own heart and still managed to stash the murder weapons under your bed, Osteen," Abernathy said.

"And there was a new hibachi grill in your garage with the same kind of charcoal we found at the murder scene. We think you were going to roast Jerry's heart on it but got interrupted."

Suddenly, the calm rational Osteen vanished again.

"It's a *setup*," he hissed, then exploded into action. He went around the table and began to pound on the door. "Help me, help me! I've been set up."

A moment later, two husky patrol officers came through the door and soon had Osteen cuffed and shackled again.

"Take him by Lakeshore again and tell the shrinks you saw him attack three police officers," Abernathy said to the patrol officer. When they were gone, he turned to me and Claiborne.

"Well, too bad about that. I for one was interested in hearing more about the esoteric aspects of the Aztec method of sacrifice," Abernathy said.

Nine

Sigmund Freud once said, "The very emphasis of the commandment: 'Thou shalt not kill,' makes it certain that we are descended from an endlessly long chain of generations of murderers, whose love of murder was in their blood as it is perhaps also in ours."

He was right. Murder is so much a part of our culture that we have broken it into degrees and created a host of legal documents debating what forms of killing are justifiable. The quotation from Freud was on my mind as I made the last stop of the day before picking up Magdala at the vets.

Tiny was sitting inside the foyer collecting the cover charge at Sammy's Place when I arrived. For a brief instant, he considered not opening the door, then thought better of it. I stepped inside and paused, letting my eyes adjust to the dimness inside.

"Is there somethin' I can help you with?" Tiny said. "Sammy went out for change."

"Nothing I can think of, Tiny."

I spotted Sadie at a table in the back corner. A car salesman-type with his tie loosened, was trying to paw her all over, but with little success as she sipped what was probably tea from a highball glass. I walked back and laid my badge case in front of him on the table.

"Take a short walk," I said.

He leaned forward, focused on the badge, then scooted his chair back clumsily. "Be back in a minute... whas' yer name?"

"Stormy," she said.

"Be back in a minute, Stormy." The man got up, staggering as he went, towards the restroom down the hall in the back.

"I hope you have a good reason for that," Sadie said. "He's with a convention out of Ohio and he has a pocketful of money."

She was wearing a pink sequined bikini and bra set and her nail polish had changed to black from green.

"Just take a minute. Do you see anyone in this picture with Jerry that you've seen before?" I handed her the picture I had taken from Jon Wyatt's dining room table. She picked it up and held it near one of the dim lights on the wall for a better look.

"The one with the strange eyes is Jed something. He came in here with Jerry one night and Jerry took me to his house once to look at a collection of swords and knives."

"Did he give Jerry anything that night?" I asked.

"Chief, he gave him a couple of things, but I don't really remember what they were. We had been smokin' dope and chewin' Jerry's pain pills, the time released ones."

"Thanks, Sadie. I'll let you get back to your customer."

"Dontcha want to know about the other one?" she asked.

"What other one, Sadie?"

"The one in the 82nd Airborne T-shirt."

"You mean Ronald Oxendine?"

"Don't know what his name is, Chief, but a week before Jerry was killed, that guy was in here drinkin' with him. It was real pleasant at first, then the guy got mad. Jerry was tryin' to calm him down. Followed him outside, then came back alone. I asked Jerry what was wrong and he said the boy was confused."

"You're sure it was the same man that's in *this* picture."

"Chief, I don't know much. But I know men. That's the guy Jerry had the argument with."

"Thanks, Sadie."

On the way out, Tiny followed me into the foyer. He put his hand on my left shoulder. "Me and you needs to get somethin' straight, Mister."

"You're right, pinhead." I snapped my right wrist and the collapsible baton I had just taken from my pocket opened as I turned inside the big man's grip. I brought it up hard and the rounded point was right under his sternum, pushing him into the wall. His eyes widened and he stopped moving. I knew the pain was excruciating.

"Listen closely, big boy. If we were dogs, you'd be a big, clumsy Great Dane and I would be a scarred old Pit Bull. Grunt if you understand me so far."

He managed to grunt.

"You strut around and your size impresses the Chihuahuas and Beagles. Now that you know what *I* am, I hope you have enough sense to get out of my way the next time you see me coming. The first time you got in my face, I let it go. This time I'm giving you good advice. If there's a third time, you don't even want to think about it. Grunt if you understand."

He grunted and I stepped back and let off the pressure. Tiny bent over at the waist, taking deep breaths, the top of his shiny head had sweat on it. I waited to see if he truly understood the circumstances, then I turned and walked out.

Magdala was lying on the floor watching my every move as I prepared a quick dinner of garden salad, microwaved whole sweet potatoes and medallions of pork tenderloin. The microwave oven, as far as I'm concerned, ranks right up there with the hot shower among civilization's comforts — at least for thawing frozen stuff and cooking veggies. Meat needs to be cooked with real heat.

When Jennifer came in through the kitchen door from the garage, Magdala didn't growl. She learns very quickly. When Jen kissed me, however, the big canine whimpered as if in pain.

"Magdala, the last thing I need in this house is a jealous bitch." Magdala's ears went up at the mention of her name and she stood to allow my beautiful *compañera* Latina to scratch her ears.

"The two of you were in the news today," Jennifer said. "All three television stations."

I answered: "It was apparently a slow news day. Are you ready to eat? If you are, I'll set the salads out. I have them chilling. I also need to butter the sweet potatoes and heat them back up."

"Let me kick off my shoes, slip into something more comfortable," Jen said.

In a few minutes we were eating slowly and sipping fresh Brazilian Arabica coffee. It was the time of day that belonged to us. On occasion we go out, but generally the evening is time we reserve for ourselves.

"How was your day today, *mi compañera?*" I asked.

"Just so-so," she answered around a bite of sweet potato and butter dusted with brown sugar. "Nothing big. Did you shoot anybody today or get sued, *muchacho?*"

"Not today," I answered, cutting off a piece of pork so tender it didn't require a knife.

"Tomorrow I have to drive to Nashville and interview an inmate at the women's prison. I expect to be back in plenty of time, but could you plan on picking up Magdala at the vet's, just in case? It closes at seven in the evening."

"When are you going to start leaving her here at the house," Jennifer asked. "She may as well start doing it since it's obvious she's here to stay."

"I thought we'd start with a shorter period, like on a weekend. I think she'll be all right but a German Shepherd with separation anxiety can do a lot of damage," I said.

"Okay, I'll plan on it. This sweet potato is fabulous. When did you start dinner?"

"An hour or so earlier. The sweet potatoes were done in the microwave. I didn't have time to bake them."

"They turned out just as well," Jen said. "Who's the inmate?"

"Her name's Carol Oxendine, aka Carol Groman, Carol Mullins and Carol Jones. She started out turning tricks when she was a kid, got hooked on painkillers and developed a habit of being in the wrong place at the wrong time. She's doing a minimum of twenty-five years for second degree murder right now."

"Sounds like a real winner. Was she involved in one of your cases?"

"Her son is a suspect in Jerry Carpenter's murder." I replied.

"Then shouldn't KPD investigators be going down to talk to her?"

"They haven't made the connection. If there isn't one, I don't want to cause this boy any problems. Having Carol as a mother is trouble enough for anyone."

"I'm glad you're not still taking over cases on the sly like you used to do in the past, Shiloh — especially since these detectives have been nice enough to keep you updated."

"If it pans out, I'll give it to them and they can take all the credit." I said.

"Nobody accused you of being a glory hound, I'm just worried about the frame of mind that almost killed you before bypass surgery — which is the mistaken belief that nothing will get done if *you* don't do it."

"This is a special case. Jerry was my friend," I said, taking my last bite of pork tenderloin.

"They're all special to you, *Jefe* Tempest."

"You may be right, but I am who I am, Jen."

"And that's why I love you, Shiloh Tempest. But you worry me to death. What do you say we take a shower and watch television in bed? Last one in is a sissy!"

Jennifer's robe hit the floor as she bolted down the hall. The "something comfortable" that she had slipped into before dinner was her skin. I got up and followed my *compañera* of twenty years, shedding clothes as I went. Magdala followed me with a puzzled expression on her long black shepherd face.

Ten

At one time there were signs at the state line to greet visitors that said, "Welcome to the Three States of Tennessee." Apparently someone decided the signs were not a good public relations tool and they went away. There are, in fact, three grand divisions, along geographical and cultural lines.

East Tennessee is Appalachian in culture and accent, a mountainous region with deep valleys. East Tennessee meets Middle Tennessee on the Cumberland Plateau and the landscape becomes mostly rolling hills and valleys.

Nearing the Mississippi River, Middle Tennessee meets West Tennessee and flattens out into delta country. About 440 miles long and 120 miles wide, it means that Knoxville and Memphis are closer to many northern cities than to each other. The three states of Tennessee sign was apt, if not politically correct.

Historically. East Tennessee — unlike Nashville and Memphis — was a Union stronghold and has been consistently Republican since the Civil War.

I had just driven my newly furbished Ford cruiser, maroon in color, over the Cumberland Plateau from Knoxville and was outside the Tennessee Prison for Women in Nashville. The Ford had been in my parking space at the garage that morning when I arrived and the fleet master was there to help me move my gear into the old cruiser that now looked new.

Apparently the engine had been rebuilt because I had to keep decelerating all the way to Nashville on I-75. There was also a new camera and laptop computer. I had enjoyed the drive and had made good time from the moment I left home until my arrival.

TPW is located near downtown Nashville. It's the State's largest women's prison, with an operating capacity of 744. Tennessee's only two women ever to be sentenced to death, Gail Owens and Christa Pike, are here. All the women are separated from the world by a 17-foot fence and five coils of razor wire. I don't like prisons or jails and I never visit unless it's important.

Even police officers are subjected to the impersonal world of corrections when they enter, no exceptions. I left my weapon and handcuffs in the cruiser but forgot about the handcuffs keys on my key ring. A guard politely took the keys and out them in a paper envelope. When I finally arrived in the visitation area, it was almost anticlimactic.

The room where I was taken to meet Carol Oxendine could have been the dayroom of a hospital. The floor is tiled and there are tables scattered through a large room, with drink and candy machines along one wall. After a few minutes, Carol was brought in and the guard who escorted her stood by the entrance out of hearing range, but within sight.

Time had not been good to Carol. I knew her to be forty-seven, but she looked sixty-five. Once she had been pretty, but years of drug abuse and time in correctional facilities had erased all signs of the girl she had once been.

When she approached, still puzzled by a visitor who could get in at a time other than regular visiting hours, I would never have recognized her.

"Carol, I'm Chief Shy Tempest from the Knox County Sheriff's Office. Do you remember me?"

Suddenly a toothless smile split her wrinkled face. "Of course, I 'member you. Didn't ya put me in jail often enough? Look's like time's treated you better'n me." She took a seat at the table where I had been waiting.

"It's all relative, Carol. I'm a man whose heart beats regularly because I have a little device buried in my stomach and my arteries have been roto-rooted a bunch of times. Just being around is something for me to brag about."

"When you worked Metro narcotics there was a city cop

named Jerry. Is he still around?" she asked. "The two of you was always nice and never took advantage like some. Ya treated me like a human being."

"I'm afraid Jerry's not with us any longer, Carol. But what I want to talk to you about concerns Jerry. Would you like a soft drink, Carol?"

"That would be nice, Shy, a Coca-Cola. It's been a while since a gentleman bought me a drink," she said, unconsciously touching her hair in a flirtatious manner. I got a drink and took it back to the table.

"Here you go, enjoy, Carol," I said, sitting back down in the plastic and chrome chair. How did you get here this time, Carol?" I knew, but I wanted her in a talkative mood.

"I got tired of bein' knocked around, Shy. I took a knife to my old man's throat while he was asleep. I thought I was goin' down for First Degree for a while, but I didn't. "Course, it might as well have been at my age."

"How's your son, Carol? His name was Ronnie, wasn't it."

"Yeah, that's his name, Shy. Last time I seen him was right before he went to ranger school. He come to see me at the Knox County Jail while I was doin' time for bad checks. Ain't heard from him since. Can't say as I blame him. I wasn't much of a mother. Ron went to the orphanage when he was eight or nine."

"I'm trying to remember who Ron's father was. Did I know him, Carol?"

"Good Lord, Shy, if you knew who Ronnie's father was, you'd have been one up on me! I was turnin' tricks and Ronnie's name coulda been *Target* because so many men had a shot at bein' his father." She chuckled at her own wit. "I looked good back then, didn't I Shy?"

"You sure did, Carol. That dark Lumbee complexion made you look exotic."

"I *knowed* there was a officer I used to talk to about bein' a Lumbee from over to Lumberton, North Carolina. It was you, wasn't it? You read history and such," she said, smiling another toothless grin.

"Yeah, it was me, Carol. And sometimes Jerry Carpenter when we picked you up for one thing or another."

"That Jerry was a nice man," she said. "Whatever happened to him, Shy."

"Somebody killed him at the old World's Fair site, Carol."

"*No!* That's where I first seen Jerry, ya know?"

"Really, you remember Jerry that far back? That was seven or eight years before we worked the Metro Unit," I said.

"They's a funny story, about that, Shy. I didn't actually *know* Jerry until you and him was with the Metro unit. But I was workin' the convention center hotel at the World's Fair Park at night, makin' more money than I ever had before. Hand over fist, I made the money."

"I bet you did, Carol," I said, encouraging her to talk.

"My mother was keepin' Ronnie then. One afternoon I took him to the World's Fair Park. It was a good day. I was takin' pictures and ever'thing else. Ronnie was a toddler and was fascinated with uniforms.

"Jerry Carpenter was standing near the Sunsphere, workin' an extra security job, I guess, when Ronnie ran up to him. Jerry picked Ronnie up and was talkin' to him and I shot a picture of the two of them.

"It was such a good picture of Ronnie that my Momma had it blowed up to an 8 x 10. When he was old enough to ask who his daddy was, I didn't figure there was any harm, so I pointed at the picture and told Ronnie that Jerry was his daddy. I'd bet Ronnie still has that picture today."

"I wouldn't doubt that, Carol." *No harm was done, at least not until the little boy went looking for his father and got the wrong answer.* "Did you ever tell Jerry about the picture?"

"No, I don't think I ever did. By the time you and Jerry started arrestin' me, my Mom had died and I'd lost custody of Ronnie. Didn't seem to be any point in mentionin' it then. Besides, I was stoned out of my mind on crack cocaine most of the time."

"I do remember *that*, Carol."

"There's times I wish I'd been a better person, but I don't

dwell on it, Shy. I'm here and this is my whole world." She looked around, a woman old before her time.

"Carol, I'm going to put some money in your account here, just for old time's sake."

"Shy, that would be nice. But I know you didn't drive all the way down here to visit an old whore just because you wanted to see me."

"Carol. You don't know any such thing." I nodded at the guard and she came over to get Carol. On the way out I stopped and left a hundred dollars in Carol's prison account — just for old time's sake.

I stopped off at the Tennessee Law Enforcement Training Academy at Donelson, Tennessee on my way back from the TPW to visit with old friends.

When I became a state certified police officer there were only a few local departments with academies. Most of us were trained at Donelson. I ended up staying for lunch and it was a little after eight that evening when I got home.

As soon as I opened the kitchen door from the garage, Magdala was licking my hand, whimpering a greeting and all but jumping up and down. I stopped and grabbed her by the head, looked her in the face and rubbed her ears. "I'm glad to see you too, Magdala."

"Shiloh," Jennifer called to me from the sunroom, "I stopped at the deli on Merchants and bought us a sandwich. You have a Reuben in the fridge and there's coffee in here."

I found the sandwich, put it on a plate and microwaved it until it was steaming again, then made my way to the sunroom. Magdala followed me and plopped down by my chair with a deep sigh.

"Magdala was quite upset when we got home and you weren't here," Jennifer said. "I had to open every door in the house so she could look. She heard your car before you turned into the driveway and ran to meet you."

"Did you miss me, Magdala?" She raised her head, ears at attention, and whimpered.

"How was your trip? Did you find anything of interest?" Jennifer asked.

"Yes, I did. It seems that Carol Oxendine raised her son to believe that Jerry Carpenter was his father. Ron Oxendine spent most of his childhood in orphanages until he joined the Army. It gave him a motive to have killed Jerry.

"I know they had an argument right before Jerry's murder. I'm guessing Ron confronted Jerry and got upset when he had no idea of what Oxendine was talking about.

"Now we have three suspects with knowledge of Aztec history *and* possible motive. Professor Wyatt was jealous and has a bad alibi. Osteen may very well have been acting out a fantasy and has no verifiable alibi. I suppose Abernathy and Claiborne will want to pull Ron Oxendine in for questioning, after I meet with them tomorrow."

"Well, I'm glad you're giving the KPD investigators the information and not trying to follow it up yourself."

"That was my intention all along," I said.

"Sometimes, Shiloh, you let your good intentions run away with you."

"I know, my love." I took a bite of the Reuben and enjoyed the texture and mix of tastes. "Great Reuben," I said. "Every bit as good as the one I had at the Carnegie Deli in New York."

"That's high praise," Jennifer said. "And this one didn't cost thirty bucks."

Eleven

Abernathy and Claiborne had arrived at Rankin Restaurant ahead of me that morning and were finishing up breakfast. Abernathy was reading the morning paper.

"No wonder you can never find a cop when you need one," I said, sliding in next to Claiborne, since he was the smaller of the two.

"Yep," Abernathy said, "cops are always at a doughnut shop or somewhere else where there's free coffee. The public believes that passionately."

The waitress came to the table with a cup and filled it with coffee. "Will you be eating this morning?" she asked.

"Do you have any doughnuts?" I asked. She looked at me in disgust and moved on to the next table.

"You shouldn't rag a waitress with a pot of hot coffee in her hand," Abernathy said, putting down the newspaper.

"How do you know I wasn't serious?" I asked, putting a spoonful of sugar into the black coffee.

"Same way she knew. You telegraph your weird sense of humor. What's up this morning?" Abernathy asked.

I passed him Mary Oxendine's folder and took a sip of coffee. "That's Ron Oxendine's birth mother. He spent most of his life in orphanages, under the impression that Jerry Carpenter was the father that had abandoned him and his mother."

"Any chance that Jerry *was* his father?" Claiborne asked.

"No. According to Carol Oxendine, she first saw Jerry when he was a rookie, working security at the World's Fair Park. He picked up her son and she shot a picture of the two of them. She never really knew Jerry until the two of us arrested her the first time for prostitution — back when there was a city-county, Metro Drug Unit."

"How did you acquire this information, Chief?" Abernathy asked.

"I showed a picture of the men in the Thursday evening study group to Sadie Hyde, the nude dancer Jerry had a thing with, to see if she'd recognize Jed Osteen. She did, but she also recognized Ron Oxendine as having had an argument with Jerry right before he was murdered."

"What picture did you show her?" Abernathy asked.

I fished the picture out of my pocket and handed it to him. He looked at it and said: "I wonder if I might get a copy of this?" I detected a note of irritation.

"Just keep that one. I lifted it from Wyatt's house the night I was there. I'm not trying to steal your thunder. I went down and talked to Carol Oxendine because I'd knew she'd talk to me. I've left it for the two of you to interview Ron Oxendine."

"All right, Chief. Point well taken. We haven't been totally forthcoming with you either," Abernathy said. "We sent two fresh cigarette butts and a fake fingernail that had broken off with a little of the nail still attached to the lab to see if DNA can be extracted.

"We don't know if they had anything to do with Jerry's death but they were in the general area and we decided to touch all bases."

"Abernathy, I've been a cop for a long time. Dominos does not tell the Pizza Hut everything it knows about pizza. I'm not offended."

Abernathy dropped his head and grinned. "Does that mean *you're* still withholding information that might be relevant?"

"Nope, you have it all. I'm just trying to save you a little grunt work. It's your case, not mine."

"We'll call you when we pick up Oxendine for questioning. The coffee's on us today."

The two of them left and the waitress came back to the table. "I see they stuck you with the check for their breakfasts — and they both ate a lot."

I threw back my head and laughed. I had been punked by two men who hadn't even been old enough to be cops when I started.

"What's funny?" the waitress asked.

"Life is funny." I looked at the bill and handed her a twenty. "Keep the change," I said.

Back at the City-County building, I went to my office and started reducing the stack of telephone messages that had accumulated on my desk and signed off on the time cards prepared by Lieutenant Phipps, who pointedly reminded me that he was tired of doing the paper work for squads of detectives since his counterpart had transferred back to patrol.

"Got a minute, Chief?" I looked up and saw Al Reagan standing in the door.

"Sure. Come in and shut the door." With the door closed, I lit up a cigarette and got out my so-called smokeless ashtray that was supposed to filter the smoke. There's not supposed to be *any* smoking in the building.

Reagan put his huge body into the straight-backed office chair. He took out a special lens paper he carried with him and cleaned his rimless glasses without speaking.

"Spit it out, Al," I said.

"It's about the lieutenant's job? What's the process, Chief? I've talked to my wife and we could use the extra money. But I haven't bid on a job since I made detective."

"I'll put in a formal request to fill the slot. The sheriff will post it for ten days under the Merit system rules. Then the sheriff, his chief deputy and I will interview everyone who applies."

"I've noticed that our lieutenants don't get out much, Chief."

"It doesn't *have* to be that way, Al. Essentially, your job would be to make sure the shifts are covered, do time cards and check out minor complaints. Once a year, you'd do evaluations."

The big man ran his hand over his thinning, short cropped hair and sighed deeply. "If you will, have the job posted and I'll bid on it," Reagan said.

"Consider it done, Al. I think you'll be an outstanding supervisor."

"Thanks, Chief." Al Reagan got up and lumbered out of the room.

As soon as he was gone, I got on the phone and called the sheriff's secretary to see if he had time to see me. After a moment she came back and said he'd be waiting for me.

On the way up, I thought of the differences between real cops and television and movie cops. I had put off being promoted for five years when I was on the street. Even under a hostile sheriff, as I was, it was with great reluctance that I finally put in a bid for detective and got it.

After a year as an investigator, the promotion to detective/ sergeant is automatic. I was even more reluctant to become a lieutenant for the same reason Reagan was so worried. Street cops want to be on the street.

The sheriff's secretary waved me in when I arrived at his office. I found him signing paperwork. He looked up and smiled. "Some day my secretary will give me her promotion to chief deputy and I'll sign it without looking. The paperwork is unending in this job and I depend on her to make sure it gets done."

Sam signed the final document, put it aside and took out his old metal ashtray and butane lighter from a desk drawer. "Give me one of your Camels," he said.

"Why, are you nervous about something?"

"Almost every time you ask to talk to me, it means a crisis. Who have you pissed off this time?" he asked.

"Nobody that I know of," I said, shaking a cigarette out and extending the pack. I lit one of my own and sat down in front of his desk.

"That's encouraging. What do you need, Shiloh?

"I'm putting in a formal request to fill my vacant lieutenant's slots. Phipps is whining about the extra paperwork."

"Reagan finally come around?" Sam asked.

"He did finally come around."

"Does he understand that he'll have competition?" Sam asked.

"He understands."

"All right, I'll have it posted today. We need to talk about your status, too."

"What about my status?"

"I'm still carrying you as a consultant. You're rapidly approaching the point where the retirement board is going to say you have to get in or get out."

"That's a big decision, Sam. If I come back full-time, my disability pay ends and if I get too sick to work again, I'll never be able to get insurance anywhere else."

"If that happens, I know for a fact that your cardiologist will re-certify you, so you don't loose your insurance or retirement."

"You've been talking to my cardiologist again."

"Only in the most general terms while John and I are playing golf. He says your overall health has *improved* since you came back to work. Let's face it, Shiloh, you were on the rocks when I came to see you with an offer to get back in the game. You *need* to work."

"Let me discuss it with Jennifer," I said.

"Okay, and take your time, as long as it's not longer than two weeks. That's when you will have made all the money allowed under your disability pension with the county."

I left Sam's office and returned to my own. After catching up on my phone messages and signing off on routine paperwork, I decided to take the rest of the afternoon off.

Fifteen minutes later, I was at Lola Parker's vet clinic where I was boarding Magdala during the day. As I entered, Lola was walking out of one of the exam rooms.

"You're here early today," she said.

"I have some heavy thinking to do, Lola, so I took off early."

"Magdala's in my private office," she said.

"Is something wrong?"

"No, she's been spending a lot of time with me. Today I trimmed her toenails and we had a little girl talk. I don't suppose there's a possibility you've decided she's too much trouble. If you have, I'll take her. You've got a once in a lifetime dog there."

"Sorry, Lola, but if the court ordered me to give her back, they'd have to send the SWAT team. When I'm off, Magdala's never more than a few feet away."

"I found a tattoo in her ear and looked it up. Magdala's the real deal. She was born in Berlin and came from a top breeder. She's a trained guard dog.

"It makes me wonder where that idiot who was abusing her actually acquired her. He says he bought her in New York. I can check if you want me to."

"I think not, Lola. If he did steal her and I knew for sure, I'd feel obligated to contact the owner. Magdala's been through enough trauma."

"I agree, Shy. She's exceptionally intelligent, even for a top-flight German dog."

Lola opened the door and Magdala ran to me, wagging her tail and whimpering a greeting. I went down to one knee and she stuck her head under my arm. She didn't do it as often, but she still remembered where she had been and what had happened to her. I represent security.

"What does Jennifer think of Magdala?"

"They get along just fine now that the ground rules have been established. The first night she jumped on our bed and tried to sleep between Jennifer and me."

"That's a female for you," Lola said.

"I think I'm going to start getting her used to staying at home, Lola. I may not bring her in tomorrow."

"Well, she's welcome anytime. We've become girlfriends." Lola leaned over and held her hand put palm up. "Later, girlfriend." Magdala raised a paw and struck Lola's palm, as if giving a high-five slap.

Twelve

Magdala was lying by the table, watching as I drained angel hair pasta to go with the marinara sauce bubbling on the stove. I had also made a small tossed salad and had French bread with garlic butter ready to toast.

The German Shepherd's ears went up seconds before the garage door began to open and Jennifer pulled in. As the door from the garage opened, Magdala got up and went to greet her.

"Why, hello Magdala," Jennifer said, stopping to stroke our new family member's head. "Did you have a good day?" Magdala whimpered an answer.

"And what kind of day did you have, *Jefe* Tempest?" Jen came over and kissed me. "Something smells good," she said.

"Just a little marinara sauce and angel hair pasta. Dinner's ready except for the toast," I answered, patting her on the bottom as she turned away.

"Let me kick off my shoes and get into a robe. You can start the toast."

I put the toast in the oven as Jen was making herself more comfortable. "I'm glad to see you're making an effort to get along with Jennifer," I said to Magdala.

She raised her head and her ears went up. Seeing that no response was needed from her, she laid her head back on her paws.

By the time Jennifer returned, dinner was on the table and I was taking the toast from the oven. "Who were you talking to?"

"I was talking to Magdala."

"Was she answering?"

"Of course." I went to the fridge and got a shaker of Parmesan cheese.

"You look like a man with something on his mind. What is it?" Jen asked.

"I must be turning transparent in my dotage," I answered.

"I share your bed, Chief Tempest. You can't hide anything from me." She took a bite of angel hair and marinara sauce. "Very good."

"The sauce is from a can," I said, twisting angel hair around my fork.

"It's still good. So what's on your mind?"

I took a bite of marinara and pasta, chewed and swallowed before answering. "I've stayed as long as I can as a consultant. In two weeks, I either have to go back full-time or quit."

"What are you going to do?" Jennifer reached for a piece of toast.

"I thought we should discuss it, Jen."

"What's to discuss? You were a wreck when you went to work on the Quinn case. Now you're functioning perfectly well. The job agrees with you."

"There's the insurance to think about and the possibility that I will end up as an invalid without a job."

"No, not really. I had one of our lawyers who handles worker's comp to do some research. If you go back, the feds pick up the next comp claim — assuming there is one."

"So you have no problem with my returning full time?"

"Shy, light of my life, I'd rather have you with me and happy for five years, than have you dragging around in misery for the next fifteen."

"In that case…" My cell phone began to play the theme from *The Sting*.

"Tempest here," I said.

"Chief Tempest, I hate to bother you at home, but we have a barricade situation with Ron Oxendine out here on Raccoon Valley Road." It was Tom Abernathy.

"Anyone hurt?" I asked.

"Not yet. I'll fill you in on what happened when you get here. The sheriff's SWAT team is already in place around the house."

"You're aware that Oxendine's a former Army ranger?"

"Try Delta Force, Chief. I saw a 1st Special Forces patch displayed in a frame on his wall while we're in there. Just come on out, we're operating on Indigo channel." The line went dead.

"I have to go out. Ron Oxendine has barricaded himself into a house and they need a hostage negotiator."

"It's been a long time since you did that, Shiloh. Couldn't someone else handle it?"

"I have insights that nobody else has. I don't want him to die."

"You mean not *before* you solve the case!" Jen's voice had taken on a sharp edge.

"I'll be back as soon as I can, Jen."

"All right, Shiloh. Magdala and I will curl up with a good book. She might as well start getting used to it. Kiss me goodbye and go. Take care, *mi amor.*"

Raccoon Valley was only one exit away from the point where I got off every day to go home.

Fifteen minutes later I was on the scene, holding up my star and ID as I worked my way to the special operations van that was being used as command center.

Captain Bill Randall, the SWAT team commander, was talking to Abernathy and Claiborne. "Captain, what's the situation?"

"So far, he's refused to answer the land line. My officers have the green light to take him out if he shows himself with a weapon."

"Change the order to only fire on *my* command or in the event that he fires on us, Captain Randall."

"This is *my* operation, Tempest," Randall said.

"It *was* your operation, I'm assuming command and acting as the negotiator. We need Oxendine alive."

Randall took the radio from his belt and keyed it.

"Captain, if you call the Sheriff, you'll be humiliated in front of everyone listening to the radio. The Sheriff will back me. Or we can keep the decision here. Tell your men they will only fire on *my* command or if Oxendine fires on us."

While Randall was reluctantly doing as I said, I went to my cruiser and put on my body armor. When I returned to the command van, I told the communications officer to ring Oxendine's land line again. After several rings, the phone was answered and the officer handed me the mobile phone.

"What?" Oxendine asked.

"Ron, this is Chief Tempest. We need to talk."

"It sounds like all of you have been talking about me already," Oxendine said.

"Ron, an investigation has to cover every base. We've talked to every male in your study group and some outside. We just need a few answers from you. Let me come in alone and talk to you."

"Let me think about it." The line went dead.

"Abernathy, tell me exactly what happened. It's going to be pitch black soon."

"Chief, we knocked on the door and told him we had some questions. He was amicable, so we went in and sat down. We told him we knew about his argument with Jerry right before he was found dead and he got a little antsy. When we asked him to come downtown with us, he agreed but said he needed to take a leak first.

"Claiborne went in and checked the bathroom for weapons and exits and we let him go in there. Somewhere, he had a baby Glock stashed. He came out, disarmed us and sent us out the door.

"Now he has *three* Glocks and I saw what looked like a modified M-14 with a scope hanging on the wall. Even if it's just semiautomatic, that's a weapon that can kill as far as the shooter can see." Abernathy said.

"This is very important, Abernathy — did either of you mention his mother?"

"No, we didn't want to set him off. We were going to get him downtown in a controlled environment and call you."

"All right." I turned to the officer in the van. "Ring Oxendine up again."

The phone was answered on the third ring. Oxendine was terse: "Talk, Chief."

"Ron, we know you're heavily armed and know how to use everything you have. This can only end one of two ways. We can talk or people are going to die."

"Are you ready to die for your mission, Chief?"

"I'd rather *live* through my mission and see us all walk away alive, Ron."

"Good answer, Chief. Walk directly to the front door. It will be unlocked. If you're armed when you get here, you die. If it's a trick, you die along with a bunch of other men who would prefer to go home. Are we clear?"

"Clear. I am about to step around the van and begin my walk. I'm wearing khaki pants and a plaid shirt with a Kevlar vest over it."

"All right," he said. "I'm waiting."

I handed Abernathy my Glock 26 pistol.

"Are you actually going in there, Chief?" The SWAT team commander asked.

"Yes, I am."

"What if he puts a 7.62 round from that M-14 between your eyes on the way up?"

"That would put you back in charge, Captain."

Only a fool is fearless. I'm not a fool, so the sweat was gathering between my shoulder blades ten feet into the hundred yard walk to Oxendine's front door. But it was a calculated risk, not foolhardiness on my part.

Besides, if he did put a round through my head, I'd never feel it or even hear the sound. I'd seen what an M-14 round does to a human head in Vietnam.

On the front porch, I paused. "Ron, I'm ready to open the front door."

"All right," he replied.

I opened the door and Oxendine was standing by the wall to my left in the dimming light, holding a pistol. I held my hands where he could see them.

"Take off the Kevlar very slowly and toss it on the floor in front of me," he said.

The Velcro straps made a lot of noise as I pulled them loose. I tossed the vest at his feet and put my hands back in front.

"Chief, you've been sweating through your shirt. Doesn't feel that hot outside to me," Oxendine said.

"It's not the heat, it's the humidity," I answered.

"No, it's the heat. It's *always* the heat. Turn completely around, lift your trousers above the ankles," he said.

He seemed very calm, but I knew his casual attitude was part of learned self-control — either that or he was insane, in which case I had made a bad call by entering.

"Okay, I didn't expect you to be carrying. Have a seat. Would you like a cup of coffee? I made it and put it in the Thermos while the detectives were busy calling the cavalry."

"Sure," I answered. "Ron, you had plenty of time and opportunity to leave with only two sets of eyes watching. Now there's no way out. Why did you do this?"

"*You* say there's no way out. But why do you think I had the skills to escape when I wanted to?" He poured a cup of coffee into the plastic Thermos top and handed it to me.

"The framed patch hanging on your wall tells me that," I answered, taking a sip of coffee.

"Did you wear the Green beanie, Chief? I figure you for a Vietnam vet and you don't strike me as a clerk — as overweight and out of shape as you are now."

"No beanie. I was with the 173rd Light Infantry on Hill 875."

"Sky Soldier. I'm impressed. I hear there were as many as five thousand dead North Vietnamese Regulars killed there."

"We thought we were going up after a company strength unit," I said, sipping my coffee again. "We didn't do it on purpose."

"How many casualties in your company?" he asked.

"The First sergeant and I were the only ones who walked back down that hill. Everyone else went on a stretcher or in a body bag."

"You earned your bones, Chief, so I'll answer. I waited around because I expected you to show up and offer to talk to me," Oxendine said.

"Where did you earn your bones, Ron? Want a sip of coffee?"

"No coffee. I was on the ground in Afghanistan near the Iranian border a few days after 9/11. I speak Farsi *and* Arabic."

"Now, *I'm* impressed. Why did they let you leave the military?

"My hitch was up and the people in the know don't screw around with men like me, Chief."

"I get your drift, Ron. What did you want to talk to me about? It would have been easier just to call me." I drained the coffee and put the cup down.

"I did answer when *you* finally called," he said.

"You were monitoring all our channels."

"People in my line of work tend to have several different skills. I wanted to talk to you about my father, Jerry Carpenter," Oxendine said.

"What do you want to know?" I decided it would be in my interest to proceed carefully.

"What kind of man was he?"

"He was one of the finest and bravest men I ever went under fire with. If Jerry Carpenter had my back, I knew my back was covered."

"What happened to him?" Oxendine asked.

"He piled up on a police motorcycle and was in intensive care for a month. He got hooked on heavyweight painkillers and never got the proper treatment for the addiction."

"Was he crooked?"

"No, he wasn't. If he'd had proper therapy, Jerry would have come back strong. But he had enemies in high places and he was drummed out instead of being treated."

"He doesn't sound like the kind of man who would abandon a wife and child, does he?" Ron Oxendine said.

"He *wasn't* that kind of man."

"Sure he was. He abandoned me and my mother when I was a baby and she ended up..."

"In the Tennessee Prison for Women," I said.

It was tense moment. I knew a slip could result in my death.

"So you knew my mother, too?"

"I *still* know your mother, Ron. I talked to her two days ago. That's why we wanted to talk to you today."

He took a deep breath and held for a few seconds, struggling for control.

"How is she?" he asked.

"She's like the rest of us, Ron. She's older, tired and full of regrets."

"What did you talk to her about?"

"I asked her if Jerry Carpenter was your father."

"What did she say?" he asked.

"She told me that when Jerry was a rookie working the World's Fair Park when you were a toddler, he picked you up and she shot a picture of the two of you. Jerry and I didn't meet your mother until years later when she got so heavy into drugs."

"Telling lies can get you killed." His voice had taken on a hard edge.

"That's why you know I'm not lying, Ron. But we can settle the issue with a simple DNA test. You're not a wanton killer. You just need the truth. Leave here with me and I give my word that we'll get the test done. We already have Jerry's DNA from the autopsy."

"The problem is, you think I killed him," Oxendine said.

"I *did* and we still have to investigate. But after talking with you, I don't believe it any longer."

"Not good enough, Chief. Step over here to the door where I can watch you from the bathroom."

For a moment I thought I was about to die and I regretted that I would never see Jennifer again, but I complied because I had no choice. He didn't shoot, though. Instead, he reached into the bathroom and I heard things moving in the medicine cabinet.

"Move back where you were," he said.

"What are you going to do, Ron?"

"Take the cellophane from around your cigarettes, Chief."

I did as he told me, moving very slowly. I saw what he had gotten from the bathroom. It was a cotton swab. He put it in his mouth and rubbed it against the inside of his cheek.

"Now hold the cellophane from the cigarettes at arm's length," he said.

I did as I was told and Ron Oxendine moved close enough to stuff the damp cotton ball into the cellophane packet.

"Now, go out the door and send my DNA to the lab," he said.

"Jerry, it will take a week minimum to get the results back. There's a SWAT leader out there who is itching to come in after you."

"Leave now, Chief. Get the results for me."

I opened the door and even though the area was lit up with floodlights, I yelled, "It's Tempest. I'm coming out alone."

The walk back to the van was as long as the walk to the house. As I stepped behind the van, there were suddenly popping sounds and what looked like muzzle flashes behind the windows of the house.

Then they were drowned out by at least ten officers opening fire with pistols, shotguns and sniper rifles. It always happens. When the first shot is fired the plan goes to hell. When there was a lull, I yelled, "Cease firing!"

After the echo from the last round died out, I turned to Captain Randall. "It's your show now Captain."

As the SWAT team was preparing to make an entrance to the house, I called out to Abernathy and Caliborne. "Do you guys have a small evidence bag?"

"Sure," Abernathy said. "Don't you want to wait until this is over?"

"It's *already* over. If Oxendine didn't have a tunnel, he probably got out while everyone else was shooting up his house. We won't see him again until ready to talk to us. I'm sure he has resources we can't imagine."

"What's the evidence bag for?" Claiborne asked.

"It's a DNA sample from Oxendine to match with Jerry's DNA to prove he's not Ron's father."

As I was putting the damp cotton swab into the envelope, the SWAT team tossed a stun grenade through Oxendine's window. There was a loud boom and flash, then the SWAT team entered. Five minutes later they were back outside and an angry Captain Randall was stalking towards me.

"Was Oxendine *really* in that house, Tempest."

"He was when I went in and came out."

"The sonofabitch set off firecrackers and apparently went out a side window during the shooting. I'm going to put the bird up and find him!"

"You won't find him, Captain. But if you did, it would end badly for whoever found him. Ron Oxendine is a breed of cat you don't want to run into in the dark."

"I don't like being played," Randall said.

"Nobody does, Captain. But he just played us all."

"Captain," Abernathy asked. "Did you notice if he left our pistols?"

"Yeah, your Glocks were laid out neatly on the coffee table," Randall answered.

"That's a relief," Claiborne said. "I wasn't looking forward to explaining *that*."

"Essentially, the only thing we have on Oxendine is assault," I said. "We can call it *aggravated* because he pointed a pistol at us. A good lawyer is going to get a combat veteran off on simple assault, with probation."

"I'm just glad we got our pistols back," Claiborne said.

Superior intellect makes a man or woman no less prone to lapses of judgment. Ron Oxendine was one of the most highly trained soldiers in the country and he had allowed an obsession to make him do stupid things.

The female astronaut who drove cross country wearing diapers to take out a romantic rival tossed away a life's work in a few hours.

It can happen to any of us. All human beings, no matter how rational most of the time, are prone to diving down rabbit holes of illogical behavior. We feel how we feel and feelings sometimes override logical behavior and compel us to do things we can't believe we did when it is over.

These thoughts were on my mind as I drove home from the old house where Ron Oxendine had overcome two trained police officers, held twenty others at bay, played me like a harmonica — and left when he was ready.

It was one of those stories of which the news media would get only a few details because cops don't like to admit they were played by somebody with better skills than their own.

Magdala met me at the kitchen door with wet, sloppy canine kisses, a wildly wagging tail and whimpering from deep in her chest. Jennifer was propped up in bed working on what appeared to be a legal brief. She was over her angry spell. My beautiful *compañera* does not dwell on pointless emotions.

"Well, since you're back in just a little over two hours, I take it you talked him into surrendering. There was nothing on the television news about anyone being killed," she said, looking at me over reading glasses.

"Oh, I talked to him, but he left when he was ready. Nobody knew he was gone until the SWAT team went in and came back out with egg on their faces."

"How did he manage that?" Jen asked, her curiosity piqued.

"He created a diversion with a couple of dollars worth of firecrackers."

"Is he apt to go on a shooting spree? Will he come after you?"

"No, he didn't want to hurt anybody. If he had, there would have been a lot of dead cops. He was Special Ops in the Army and we were out of our league tonight."

"What did he want?" Jennifer asked.

"He wanted to talk to me about Jerry Carpenter."

"Did you tell him the truth?" Jen asked.

"Yes, but he didn't believe it. He gave me a DNA sample to compare with Jerry's and said he'd get back with me."

"You were *that* close to him?"

"Yeah, I went in and talked to him a while. We had a nice conversation."

"Shiloh, even if I didn't spend my days reading legal briefs, I watch cop shows on television. Negotiators don't let themselves be taken hostage!" Jennifer's face had gotten a bit flushed.

"Every case is different, Jen."

"A negotiator is supposed to remain dispassionate, Shiloh."

"Jen, if I had remained aloof and dispassionate, a lot of people could have died. Have you ever changed strategy during a trial because you knew it was the right thing to do?

Or have you ever departed from a well thought out prepared closing argument because you read the jury and knew it would work? That's what I did tonight."

"Touché, *Jefe*. Are you about ready for bed?"

"Are you still upset?"

"Not with you, Shiloh. I knew what I was getting when I got into your bed the first time. I'm upset with myself for becoming a weak woman."

"You're not weak, Jen. You're just passionate. And I knew what I was getting when I took up with a twenty-year-old Latina firebrand."

Magdala had been intently listening to us from the foot of the bed. When she felt the tenseness leave the room, the big German Shepherd relaxed, sighed deeply and lay down with a loud moan on the floor beside the bed. When we both laughed, her ears went up briefly, then she closed her eyes and went to sleep.

Thirteen

The wife was thirty-eight years old, her hair bleached platinum, a size eighteen who had probably been a size six when she graduated from high school.

The blouse she was wearing was white with flowers embroidered on the front and her denim skirt was also embroidered with flowers. It looked as if she might have bought the outfit at a Cracker Barrel restaurant after breakfast one morning.

The husband was approximately the same age, wearing a mullet haircut straight out of the nineteen-seventies, short on top and long in the back.

He was dressed in a Western style shirt, blue jeans and cowboy boots with metal caps on the toes. The couple went together. Both were working hard at holding on to an indignant expression.

They had come in to make a complaint on John Freed, one of my best detectives. The alleged incident had occurred when John was working an off-duty job as a plainclothes security officer at a department store. As his supervisor, I had to interview them and make a determination as to whether he should be suspended pending an internal affairs investigation.

I turned on my micro cassette recorder, gave the date, place and time, then said, "This is an interview conducted by Assistant Chief Shiloh Tempest of the Knox County Sheriff's Office concerning an alleged act of misconduct by Detective John Freed of this department while he was working off-duty as a security officer. The complainant is Betty Sue Whaley and her husband, Donald A. Whaley, is present.

"Mr. and Mrs. Whaley, do you understand that this interview is being taped?"

"Yeah, we understand it," Don Whaley said, "but there ain't no *alleged* to it. Your detective felt my wife up and tried to get her to have sex for him to drop the made-up shopliftin' charge."

"Mr. Whaley, all misconduct and crime is *alleged* until it's proven, including your wife's shoplifting charge. I'm sure you can appreciate that."

He snorted contemptuously and crossed his arms.

"Mrs. Whaley, will you tell me in your own words what happened that day?"

"I was there at the store, shoppin' for baby clothes for my little grandson, Billy, and decided to look for some underwear for myself. While I was in that section, all of a sudden this here guy, Freed, grabbed me by the arm and said, 'You have to come with me, bitch.'

"I ast him why and he said, 'Because I said so!' Then he dragged me by the arm to the security office..."

"Don't forget that he pushed you through the door and almost made you fall down, Betty Sue." Don Whaley said.

"Yeah, he said, 'Git in there, bitch,' and shoved me so hard I almost fell on my face. Then he slammed the door and said, 'What the hell do you mean stealin' them panties?' I ast him *what* panties? Then he pointed to a package of three pairs of panties that was already on the table when we got there."

Betty Sue took a handkerchief from her purse and dabbed at the corner of her eyes. "He told me to sit down, then grabbed my hair and said, 'Bitch, you're goin' to jail for a long, long time unless me and you work somethin' out.'

"I ast him what he meant and he put his hand down my blouse and under my bra and pinched my left nipple. Then he said, 'You *know* what I mean, Bitch.'

"I'm a God fearin' Christian woman and I told him he'd just have to put me in jail because I don't cheat on my husband and I don't commit adultery!

"Then when he saw that he couldn't git what he wanted, he wrote me a citation for shopliftin' and said I'd have to go to the jail and be booked before court.

"It was awful," she said, "bein' dragged through that store and molested when I didn't do *nothin'* wrong."

"I can see how such an act would be deeply disturbing," I said. "I suppose even seeing Detective Freed fired wouldn't make you feel any better, but that would be all I could offer to do in such a case if the complaint were found to be true."

"Well, you wouldn't necessarily have to *fire* him," Donald Whaley said. "If he was to apologize and a *settlement* was offered, we might be willin' to forget about it."

We had reached the central point of the conversation.

"The county couldn't condone this type of act or admit responsibility, so if you made a settlement it would have to be with Detective Freed. As you know cops don't make a lot of money."

"If he could scrape up about five thousand dollars, that would probably do it. And he'd have to drop the shopliftin' charge," Whaley said.

"That doesn't seem like much for what your wife says happened. Mrs. Whaley would *you* agree to a five thousand dollar settlement?"

"Yeah, I'll never be able to git it out of my mind, but the officer's probably done some good in his time. For five thousand dollars, I'd accept his apology," she said.

"Just be absolutely certain I understand, the two of you would accept five thousand dollars in exchange for dropping the complaint against Detective Freed?"

"Yes," they said in unison.

"Would the two of you direct your attention to the television mounted on the wall. I have a recording I'd like to show you."

Both of them fell silent as I turned on the television and DVD player with my remote control. It showed Betty Sue Whaley, surrounded by lingerie looking furtively around before dropping a package into her large purse.

A few moments later, John Freed approached her and appeared to whisper and point towards the back of the store, without touching her.

The scene shifted to the security office, where the empty table was in plain view. Betty Sue came through ahead of John and both took seats. He reached into her purse and placed the package of panties on the table between them. The open door was clearly in view of the camera's range with employees moving boxes in the background.

"Mrs. Whaley," John Freed said, "is this the first time you've ever been charged with shoplifting?" The sound quality was not great, but their voices could be clearly heard.

"No, it's the third time," she said.

"I'm going to write you a citation rather than take you into custody, but you will have to appear at the Knox County jail to be fingerprinted and booked before your court date."

"Turn it off," Betty Sue said. "*Just turn it off*!"

I picked up the remote and paused the picture. "I'm guessing you don't want your husband to see you bare your breasts, then offer to get naked and perform oral sex on Detective Freed. Is that correct?"

"I'm out of here!" Donald Whaley stood up.

"Sit down, Whaley! I have a recording of you conspiring with your wife to commit extortion."

He sat back down. Betty Sue was crying some genuine tears.

"I also have evidence that your wife committed a Class C felony by knowingly making a false report. You might eventually convince a judge or jury that *you* spoke out of ignorance, but if I charge you, you'll still have to make bail. Your wife, on the other hand, has convicted herself for certain.

"You've come in here and placed a fine police officer's career in jeopardy. I would have believed him even *without* the recording because I know him to be a decent and honorable man. Honor and reputation are all a cop has. Detective Freed is out there every week working extra jobs so he can afford to stay in law enforcement!"

"If it had been left up to me today, you'd both be in handcuffs on your way to a cell. But I left it to Detective Freed to decide and he's not only a good man, he's a compassionate man. The deal I'm offering you is to apologize to *him* before you leave. It's that or jail.

"On your way out, stop by internal affairs and tell them... Tell them whatever you want. But be aware that if I hear anything else about this bogus complaint, I'll personally sign warrants and that recording of Betty Sue offering to prostitute herself over five dollars worth of panties will be played in open court.

"Now get out of my office!"

Most people find it difficult to believe that their friends and neighbors walk into a police department and lie in order to get a cop fired or to extort money.

The same people also find it hard to believe that people in police custody will bang their faces against the pavement or the screen in a police car to make a case for police brutality. But it happens every day. I've had people try to get me fired over twenty-five dollar traffic ticket on an offense for which they were guilty.

Fifteen minutes after the Whaleys left, John Freed knocked on my door.

"Come on in, John."

The thin, wiry redhead, who was noted all over the county for his courtesy and habit of never cursing, came into my office, walked up to my desk and put out his hand.

I took his hand and he gave me a firm grip. "Chief, thanks for bailing me out."

"John, I didn't *bail* you out. You did everything by the book and I would have believed you even without the security video."

"I know you would, Chief. But IAD wouldn't have believed me and that complaint would have gone into my file. You persuaded them to apologize, then withdraw the complaint and saved me a lot of trouble," Freed said. "It hasn't always been that way, you know."

"I know it well, John."

"Some of us have been talking. We know you only took this job temporarily, but we'd all like to see you stay permanently."

"John, you can thank Sheriff Sam Renfro for the changes. I just work for him. He makes policy here."

"Did you know you have a nickname now, Chief?" Freed asked. "Our last chief of detectives, Rosenbaum, was called

'Chief Stiffy.' Your nickname is 'Chief Bear' because you fight for your officers like a momma bear protecting her cubs."

"I didn't know that, John." I was touched but, of course like any macho cop, I did my best to hide it.

"I told the rest of the guys I'd pass it along, for whatever it's worth." Freed wouldn't look me in the eye because real men don't give compliments.

"John, that matter is under discussion between me, the sheriff and my *compañera*, Jennifer. I *will* factor in what you've said when I make a decision. Thank you."

My cell phone rang out the theme from *The Sting*. "Tempest, here."

"Chief Tempest, this is Tom Abernathy. Would it be possible for you to meet me for lunch?"

"I can manage that. Say where."

"How about the Falafel Hut?"

"I'm not a vegetarian but I do like falafel sandwiches, hummus and baba ganoush. I can wrap things up here and be there in half an hour."

"My treat. See you in thirty minutes, Chief."

It was a short drive to the Falafel Hut in the University of Tennessee area. The food is great. I don't care for their soup but everything else is first class. I went in and took a seat and Abernathy wasn't far behind me. He came in carrying a folder and sat down across from me.

"I appreciate your meeting me on short notice," he said.

"Not a problem," I said. "Where's your sidekick today?"

"He's taking a couple days off."

"What's on your mind, Abernathy?" I asked.

"First off, we did an intense canvas of Professor Wyatt's neighborhood. A couple of neighbors remembered that he came in late, at least midnight, the night Jerry Carpenter was killed. That classic Austin-Healey he drives makes a distinctive sound, so I tend to believe the neighbors.

"I'm going to try and get a search warrant for Wyatt's house and vehicle and sweat him tomorrow. I thought you might want to be there.

"My Chief is pushing me to charge Jed Osteen with murder, so I'm going to try and get the warrants before I'm forced to charge him."

"Why does Hodge want you to charge Osteen now, while he's at Central State Hospital being evaluated?"

"I suppose he needs an excuse to call a press conference."

"Judge Clement might give you the search warrant based on Wyatt's lie and the fact that he has weapons similar to the ones that killed Jerry, but I can't think of another who would. It's thin, Tom."

"I know that, Chief, but I really like him for this murder, even more than Ron Oxendine, though I'm not ruling him out."

"You're too good an investigator to rule out anyone at this point, Abernathy."

"I appreciate that, Chief. I've sorta felt like an amateur watching you work this case, I have to admit."

"I'm old and have learned not to stick my hand into the fire or get in a hurry. You'll get there. Count me in tomorrow, if you don't think it will get you in hot water."

"Hodge is going to Chattanooga to give a speech. He'll be gone all day tomorrow. Even he's not stupid enough to try and drive back after he drinks as much as he always drinks."

A pretty young girl of obvious Middle Eastern ancestry came to the table and took our orders. I ordered a falafel sandwich and baba ganoush, a very spicy eggplant dish. Along with falafel, which is a chick pea and or fava bean mixture, usually served in the shape of meatballs, it's a perfect protein meal with no meat.

We sat quietly for a few minutes. I had a distinct feeling that Abernathy had something else he wanted to discuss. Finally, I just said, "Spit it out, whatever's on your mind, Tom."

"I guess I'm pretty transparent," he said grinning like a child caught misbehaving.

"Not particularly. I've been dealing with people about thirty years longer than you have, Tom."

"I've told you that I've read your books, all of them, in fact. Well, I'm... like really into fiction. And, I... and feel free to say no..."

"You've written a book or you're writing a book. Correct?"

"Right. I don't know why I had so much trouble getting it out."

"I do, Tom. You're about to ask me to give you an opinion on your writing. When we write we bare our souls. And I'm not a distant magazine editor you'll never meet. You still have to look me in the eyes after I read — *if* I read it."

"That's about the size of it, Chief." I suddenly realized that Tom Abernathy bore a strong resemblance to Denzel Washington.

"So you're not saying *no* right off the bat?"

"I'm not saying *yes*, either. This is not something to be taken lightly because if I read what you've written, I still have to look you in the eyes, also. You may be the best writer since Kurt Vonnegut, but you're probably not."

"No, I don't believe *that*."

"You'd *better* believe it. You never want to say it out loud, because people will resent it if you are and they'll laugh at you if you're not. But if *you* don't believe you're a superb writer, you might as well quit now."

"So you *will* read it?" he said.

"Not until we've discussed it. I would prefer to send you to a friend of mine who teaches small, private classes. He won't lie to you but he'll let you down gently if he thinks you don't have what it takes. I, on the other hand, am not diplomatic.

"If I read your manuscript, I will tell you *exactly* what I think and we probably won't be friends any longer — even if you believe me.

"I am of the opinion that good writing can't be taught. If you're good, I could teach you to be better, but I won't because I'm not an editor or a teacher. The best thing would be for you to see my friend and there's no risk involved for our relationship."

"What if I *don't* believe you?" he asked.

"If you don't believe me, then you'll go on writing the same kind of crap, but you still won't like me for being disrespectful to your work."

"Sounds like you've had a lot of experience at this," he said with a rueful smile.

"Every professional writer has had the experience, over and over again, Tom. And the odds are that I'm *not* going to be able to tell you that you're a superb writer because they are as scarce as hen's teeth. Writing is really not something you do unless you're compelled to do it."

"You have the name of your friend handy?" he asked.

I took out one of my business cards and wrote my friend's name and number on the back of it. "It's a wise decision, Tom. I like you and hope we'll be working together in the future."

Magdala met me at the kitchen door and sniffed the plastic grocery bag from Ingles. I stopped to pat her head and she licked my hand. She had adjusted well to staying in the house, the perfect family member.

"You smell that ground meat don't you, Magdala?" Her ears went up. "But you can't eat raw meat because it can make you sick."

I filled Magdala's drinking bowl with fresh water, put a top-grade dry dog food in her food bowl and set both of them in the floor by the kitchen table. She went to the bowl, sniffed the dry dog food and looked longingly towards the grocery bag.

"Eat up, Magdala, we have to keep you thin and svelte." She sighed deeply to show her general disgust but then began to eat greedily.

I washed my hands and put twelve ounces of ground chuck, a half pound of lean ground pork and a half pound of ground turkey into a skillet to brown. By that time Magdala was ready for her afternoon pit stop. I turned the heat down low and went out with her.

She ran around checking out the yard and looking for the perfect place to relieve herself. A squirrel caught her attention but she had learned in just a few days that chasing them was pointless. When she was finished, we went back in. I had plans for a fence and a doggie door but hadn't got around to it.

I stirred the browning meat, went to the bedroom and changed into blue jeans, Rockport walking shoes and a loose short sleeve shirt. Back in the kitchen, I got down to serious meal preparation, beginning with putting on a pot of Ecuadorian coffee, a strong brew.

Soon I had a small bowl full of diced bell peppers, onions and a large clove of garlic, crushed, which I dumped into the skillet. Then I added pure chili powder, cumin, paprika and a little cayenne pepper, and left the meat to cook. I diced a tomato, washed lettuce, tore the leaves into small pieces and put them on a platter.

I drained the meat to get rid of what little fat there was, put it back into the skillet and poured in a half cup of fresh coffee. While the coffee was cooling down, I got out a bag of corn chips, sour cream, mild salsa for Jennifer and a jar of *jalapeños* for me.

The meal was a rip-off of the Petro — layers of lettuce and tomato, corn chips and sour cream and chili — which first made its debut at the 1982 World's Fair here in Knoxville, served in small bags of Fritos. Petros are no longer served in bags but the ingredients are still the same.

When I was a kid, there were a couple of hamburger chains, similar to Krystal, but most restaurants served local cuisine. I was eighteen before I ate a pizza and older than that before I had any kind of Mexican food, except for chili, and it was Tex-Mex style.

Today, burritos, tacos and enchiladas are as familiar to Appalachian youth as milk gravy and biscuits. My son feasted on what once were exotic dishes to me as he grew up, and viewed it as normal.

By the time my lovely in-house Latina came home from a hard day of lawyering, I was putting everything on the table and Magdala was lying in her usual spot, black snout in the air, sniffing all the delicious smells.

"Something smells good," Jennifer said, stopping to slip her shoes off. The woman would go to work barefoot if it were allowed. She hates shoes. She stopped long enough to kiss me and then pat Magdala on the head before going back to get into a robe. Jen doesn't like clothes a lot, either.

A few minutes later, we were enjoying a simple but tasty and nutritious meal and sipping good coffee.

"How was your day, *amor*? Did you solve any murders — shoot anyone?"

"No, the last few have been smoking guns, not whodunnits." I ignored the "shooting" question. "How about you. Did you get any dangerous scumbags back on the street?"

"No, but the preliminary hearing on Jorge Chávez is coming up in a couple of days," she said. "We need to talk about it."

"Sorry, but I can't discuss an open case with a defense attorney."

"Shiloh, don't be a jerk. I'd send it straight to the grand jury, but Jorge can't make bail. Let's at least talk about it."

"Sorry, Jen, but he tried to kill me and he's going away if I have anything to do with it. I don't think the judge is going to look favorably on what he did."

"Come on, Jorge comes from a country where the police are feared by citizens for good reason. You scared him and he overreacted," Jennifer said. "I can't believe you're being so stubborn."

"The next time he *overreacts* he might have a nine millimeter instead of a .25 caliber, Saturday night special and he might actually kill a cop."

"He's very sorry about shooting at you. We're willing to plead out and let him serve a few months in jail."

"Don't forget that he's very religious, too. You should have heard him praying after I shot him."

"Shiloh, this man hasn't had a lot of breaks in his life. He's basically not a violent man and he has a great work ethic."

I went on eating and didn't answer.

"Oh all right! I'll ask for a continuance and wait for you to change your mind."

"I'm not going to change my mind."

"Never say never," she said.

Fourteen

My cell phone rang the next morning, just as I arrived at my office. "Tempest here."

"Chief, this is Abernathy. I got the warrant to search Wyatt's house and car. I'm going to try and pick him up while Claiborne directs the search."

"Call me when you're on the way back to headquarters and I'll meet you there, Tom."

"Gotcha covered, Chief."

The Fifth Amendment is the least understood of all the safeguards in the Constitution. If word ever gets out that people really *don't* have to talk to cops, it will become difficult to enforce the law. Occasionally, you run into somebody who *really* does understand it and it's very frustrating.

Even lawyers tend to spill their guts when brought in for questioning, and they should know better. It's covered in law school, I'm sure. Most people, however, when told they're being taken in for questioning, go right along.

If John and Jill Q. Citizen simply said, "I don't want to talk to you," the officer would be faced with either making an arrest or going on his or her way.

The police can detain somebody for a reasonable amount of time if an investigation is in progress, but he or she still doesn't *have* to say a word. Abernathy was on his way to run a bluff on Professor Wyatt, hoping the searches of his house or car would turn some real evidence or his conscience would get the better of him.

"There is a strong urge in normal people to confess their sins and feel better. It is, of course missing in sociopaths and psychopaths.

Since confessions are often obtained through interrogation, police officers are at a distinct disadvantage if they can't get the subject to talk. Abernathy was operating under the hope that Wyatt would be like *most* people. If he said he didn't want to come in, there wasn't enough evidence to arrest him.

"Morning, Chief." I looked up and Freed and Reagan were both at my door. Reagan was carrying fresh coffee and Freed had a bag which I knew from past experience would contain some type of breakfast biscuit.

"Come in, Detectives. What's in the bag, John?"

"Bacon, egg and cheese biscuits, Chief. They were on sale, two for two dollars. Reagan and I thought we'd bring you some like the old days when we were working the Quinn murder."

"Both of you drag up a chair and we'll use my desk as a table," I said.

"Here's a fresh coffee, one sugar," Reagan said.

I thanked him and in a moment we were all munching cop soul food, pork and eggs with biscuits. Not so long ago, before I was chief and the three of us worked out of a cramped office, the biscuits and coffee had been a morning ritual. I had missed it.

"Chief, I know John already thanked you, but you should know that what you did for him was appreciated by all of us. We haven't been used to fair treatment."

"Then you guys need to thank the sheriff. He makes policy and the policy is that cops get the benefit of a doubt."

"All the same, Chief, we appreciate your part in it."

"It's been noted. Thank you," I said.

Reagan finished his biscuit, took a pack of lens cleaning papers from his jacket pocket, then took off his rimless glasses and cleaned them thoroughly. I knew he was about to say something he deemed important, so I sipped my coffee and waited.

"The lieutenant position was posted this morning," he finally said.

"And you are going to bid on it, I hope, Al."

"It depends," Reagan said.

"On what?" I asked.

"On whether my Chief of Detectives decides to take his job permanently."

"Al, you should bid on it, whether I stay or not."

"I don't know, Chief. I like my job and I like working for you, but I may not like whoever takes your place. If you leave, I'm going to stay where I am."

"Al, I'll tell you what I told John yesterday. My future here is being discussed with Sam Renfro and Jennifer. I honestly don't know what I'm going to do."

"That's fair enough, Chief. But what I do *still* depends on what you do," the big detective said.

My cell phone rang and saved me from further discussion. "Tempest here."

"Chief, Professor Wyatt and I are on the way to headquarters," Abernathy said.

"I'm on my way, Tom." I closed the phone. "Gentlemen, I thank you for breakfast and for your kind words, but I have to go talk to a man about a murder."

Fifteen minutes later, I got off the elevator at the floor occupied by criminal investigations at KPD headquarters in the Safety Building. Abernathy waved to me from the doorway of the squad room. He had decided not to put Wyatt in the interrogation room, which was probably a good idea. Some people respond better outside the box.

When I entered the squad room, it was empty except for Abernathy and Jon Wyatt and the detective had just put a cup of coffee in front of the professor.

"Chief, I'm glad you could make it." Abernathy said.

I shook his hand and extended my hand to Jon Wyatt. He took my hand but was obviously not happy to be there. It's understandable. I pulled a chair up from another desk and sat down.

"I still don't understand why you couldn't talk to me in my office," Jon Wyatt said.

"Professor Wyatt, I've explained that. I didn't want to put you under a cloud. It's better here and your colleagues and students won't have to wonder why you're talking to the police," Abernathy said.

"Oh all right, but there's a grad student teaching my first class, right now. Let's get this over with," Wyatt said.

"Like I said before, Professor, we have a couple of things to clear up. But I need you to read and sign this Miranda waiver. It's just a formality so nobody can say we interrogated you with a rubber hose." Abernathy smiled pleasantly.

Wyatt picked up the waiver, read it, and signed that he had been advised of his rights and was waiving them.

"All right, Professor, you told us you went home early the night Jerry Carpenter was killed. But two of your neighbors say you didn't get in until after midnight."

"How would my neighbors know when I got home? I haven't spoken two words with any of them since I moved there."

"That Austin-Healey Sprite you drive — beautiful automobile, by the way — has a very distinct sound, Professor. One of the neighbors said you woke her up that night and she looked at her clock. The other one said he was still up, but you have also awakened him on occasion because your car's so loud."

I watched his eyes darting around as he realized he had been caught in a deception. He did what most people do when they are caught lying — the rich, the poor, the intelligent and the stupid — which is to lie some more.

"Come to think of it, I *did* go out around midnight to get pipe tobacco. That's what my neighbors heard."

"Jon, I wouldn't think an all night market would have that expensive blend you smoke," I said.

"They don't, but I'm a nicotine addict and I bought something to get me through until the next morning," Wyatt said.

"What brand did you buy?" Abernathy asked.

"I don't know, for God's sake! It was cheap but it had nicotine in it."

"Was Jerry Carpenter ever in your car, Professor?" Abernathy asked.

My ears perked up at that point. Had Claiborne called before my arrival with information I didn't know about.

"No." Wyatt took out a white handkerchief and mopped his forehead.

"What's your relationship with Professor Clark?" Abernathy asked.

"We're friends and colleagues," he said, scratching at his Vandyke beard, as if he had fleas. Wyatt was definitely becoming uncomfortable.

"We hear you and Professor Clark were bedmates before Jerry Carpenter came along and screwed up everything," Abernathy said. "Did it piss you off, Professor, to know that the woman you love was sleeping with an uneducated, alcoholic ex-cop?"

"*You* said she's the woman I love, not I. Deborah and I are adults and neither of us has a claim on the other," the flustered professor said.

"The night I attended your study group, you were watching out the window when Deborah Clark made a pass at me. I was glad, looking at your expression, that you weren't behind me with a club," I said.

"I believe you love that woman, and it's nothing to be ashamed of. She threw you over for an illiterate ex-cop, for God's sake!"

"I don't like the tone of this conversation," Wyatt said. "Maybe I need a lawyer."

"Maybe you do, Professor. If I had something to hide and the police were questioning me, *I'd* certainly want a lawyer. It's your call," Abernathy said.

"I have nothing to hide!" Wyatt said.

"It's still your right to call a lawyer or stop talking anytime you want. Of course, as you said, the quicker we get this over with, the quicker you'll be back in class."

"I'm fine," Wyatt said.

"Was Jerry Carpenter ever in your car, Professor?"

"You've already asked that and I've already told you he never was."

"I already asked that? I'm sorry," Abernathy said.

"Professor, what kind of participation did Jerry Carpenter exhibit on the nights he joined your study group?" Abernathy asked.

"Well, he was obviously intelligent, but his questions tended to be naive. He was generally polite." Wyatt said.

"Did Deborah Clark go home with Jerry the first night he attended one of your informal gatherings?" Abernathy asked.

"I have no idea," Wyatt said.

"Jon, Jon," I said. "You would've known if Deborah had left with me the night I was there because you watched us from the window. Are you trying to say you didn't know they were in the sack together that first night. Everyone else knew it."

Before Wyatt could respond, Abernathy asked another question: "Do you know where Jerry Carpenter lived, Professor?"

"Of course not! How would I know where he lived?"

"Was Jerry Carpenter ever in your car, Professor Wyatt?" Abernathy asked again.

"That's the third time you've asked that question. Why do you keep asking me if he was ever in my car?" Wyatt's face had become flushed.

"I kept hoping you would tell the *truth* professor. Our forensics team just found a Saint Michael's medallion in your car. A lot of cops wear them, and I bet if we ask Chief Tempest, he'll be able to tell us whether or not Jerry had one, and maybe even describe it," Abernathy said. "Can you do that Chief?"

"It was gold. Jerry borrowed mine to have his cast." I reached under my collar and pulled out my medallion. "Mine is silver, but otherwise, it's identical to Jerry's." *I had been right, Abernathy had received a call and had not been able to tip me off in front of Wyatt.*

"The team also found pictures in your house of Jerry Carpenter and Deborah Clark going in and coming out of Jerry's apartment," Abernathy said.

"Oh yeah," Abernathy said as if remembering an inconsequential matter, "and that medallion found in your car appears to have blood on it and the forensics team says it appears that there's a little, tiny bloodstain on the passenger seat in your Austin-Healey. Is there anything you want to tell us Professor Wyatt?"

The flush in Jon Wyatt's face had visibly drained like mercury in a thermometer, making his neatly trimmed Vandyke appear darker than normal. I would have bet the next word out of his mouth would have been "lawyer," but it wasn't.

"I... Jerry came to my house one evening about an hour early for the meeting. He asked for a ride in my car. He didn't fasten his seatbelt and when I had to stop to keep from hitting a cat, Jerry hit his face on the dash and got a nosebleed. That's probably when he lost his medallion."

"And the pictures, Professor?" Abernathy asked.

Jon Wyatt sighed deeply and shrugged. "Obviously, I took them."

"Why?" I asked him.

"Morbid curiosity," he answered. "I was trying to find out why she went with him instead of staying with me the way she used to do before he showed up."

"You were jealous,' Abernathy said.

"I suppose I was," Wyatt admitted.

"Jerry already had the fancy Aztec sword and the obsidian knife. How hard was it to entice him to the World's Fair Park that night?" Abernathy asked.

"I was never at the World's Fair Park with Jerry."

"Come on, Jon. The hard part's already out of the way," I said, "You were jealous, the oldest motive since Cain killed Abel.

"You lured Jerry out there planning to frame Jed Osteen from the beginning and he played right into your hands with his theory about a sacrifice to the Sun god.

"When it was done, you walked into Osteen's house because everyone knows he never locks the door, and you stashed the evidence under his bed."

"I did *not* kill Jerry Carpenter," he said, tiredly.

"Professor, the story about taking Jerry for a ride and his

subsequent nosebleed would have been more plausible if you had told us in the first place," Abernathy said. "Lying about not knowing where Jerry lived, didn't help your credibility much."

"I was embarrassed about following them," Wyatt said. "I was afraid it would throw suspicion on me if you knew he'd been in my car."

"You were absolutely right," Abernathy told him. "Where were you the night Jerry was killed Professor? If you have a valid explanation this is the time to tell us."

"Am I under arrest?" Wyatt asked.

"No, but as they say in the movies, don't leave town, Professor, in case we need to ask you any further questions."

"Anything else you need to ask can be addressed to my lawyer — when I hire one," Wyatt said, standing up. His knees were visibly trembling.

"Get on the elevator we came up on, Professor. Without a key, the lobby is the only place it will stop," Abernathy told him.

We watched him leave, shoulders sagging. When the elevator doors closed, Abernathy turned to me. "Why do they talk without a lawyer?"

"They think they're smarter than we are." I replied. "You think he did it?"

"Probably. At least we got enough to keep Frank Hodge from charging Osteen or anyone else until we have more."

"We still can't connect anyone to the scene of the murder, you know."

"I know Chief. I hope we'll have DNA results back soon from the cigarette butts or the fingernail to match someone. Otherwise, whoever we charge, we'll be going to court with circumstantial evidence, which I do not like and district attorneys do not like."

Traffic was fairly light on I-75 North as I drove home that afternoon, intending to take a nap, play with Magdala for a little while, then cook a light dinner. I was passing Callahan Road when the cell phone rang. "Tempest here."

"What's up, Chief Tempest?"

"We just got through putting Professor Wyatt through the wringer. Where are you Ron. How did you get my cell phone number?" I asked.

"Does it matter how I got it?"

"Not really, I guess."

"Chief Tempest, as much as I'd like to please you, I can't tell you where I am. And I'm on a disposable phone. Are my test results back yet?"

"No, Ron, the results are not back yet. In fact the results of the crime scene DNA that went out several days before yours isn't back. It's not like on television. We have to wait our turn."

"What am I charged with, Chief?"

"You could have been charged with aggravated assault for threatening the two KPD officers and me with a weapon, but I didn't sign a warrant and to my knowledge neither the KPD guys. Nobody else saw you do anything, Ron."

"Chief, you wouldn't try to con me, would you?"

"I would for the right reason. Right now, there's no reason. We really did just want to talk to you, not arrest you."

"I'm still a suspect, though. Right?"

"That you are, Ron. But we've got two others we like better than you for the murder," I told him.

"Who would that be, Chief ?"

"Sorry, Ron. I can't discuss that with you — and I can't clear you until you come in and talk to us."

"Fair enough, Chief. I'll call you. The rest of the time this phone will be turned off."

"All right, Ron. If that's the way you want to play it."

"You *do* understand that I can vanish, don't you? You won't even find my prints in the Department of Defense data bank."

"I assumed as much. But why give up being who you are if you don't have to? Obviously, who you are has some importance to you, Ron."

"When you catch the killer, I'll come in. But I can chew off my leg to get out of a trap, if I have to."

"I hope you don't have to, Ron."

"Chief, it took a lot of *cojones* for you to walk through my door the other night. Why did you do it?

"It was a calculated risk. I didn't want anyone to die."

"People die every day," he said.

"Not on my watch, Ron," I said. Then the phone went dead.

Fifteen

Several years ago a serial rapist stalked prostitutes in Knoxville for months. All the ladies of the night knew who he was, what he was doing and how he was doing it but they never told the police. Eventually he became a serial killer.

There were many points at which he could have been prevented from making that transition.

Any of the prostitutes who had been raped at knifepoint could have stopped him by just turning him in. They were more afraid of the police than a serial rapist, however.

The penalty for prostitution is light, but an arrest takes a girl off the street, costs her money and cuts her off from her narcotics. In a way, it's understandable why the prostitutes never told anyone.

A detective in a nearby county might have well have prevented the man ever having become a serial rapist to begin with, but for an investigator's sin of which he was guilty. He was a good cop who voluntarily came forward when he found out what had happened, but it was too late by then.

Long before the first murder, the man who became a serial killer picked up a young European woman touring this country. She walked out of the bus station in Knoxville, looking for a ride to the resort town of Gatlinburg. An ordinary looking man in a pickup truck said he would take her.

Instead, he took her to the back roads of Dolly Parton country, strung her up to a tree limb by her arms, then raped, sodomized and tortured her for hours, telling her all the time he was going to kill her. In the end, he did not. He left her naked and terrified by the road. Eventually, a detective interviewed her and she described a medallion worn by her rapist.

It just so happened that the detective was working another rape in which the rapist had worn the same type of medallion. The detective knew the identity of that rapist and *assumed* that the same man had raped the European girl. He never looked for a second rapist and the girl went back to Europe.

When the detective read about the serial killer in Knox County, he realized what he had done and called the Knox County detectives to tell them about the rape of the European woman. The Knox County detectives went to the serial killer and said, "Tell us about the young European woman." He looked at them for a moment and casually said: "She was for practice to see if I could really do it."

An investigator can *never* assume. What we think we know is the enemy of truth. Developing scenarios, exercising the imagination during an investigation is crucial. No investigator, however, can ever let a scenario or theory get in the way of evidence. A conclusion is where the thinking process ends.

Real trials bear little resemblance to the ones shown on television; real investigations bear even less resemblance to the television variety. Remember the *Columbo* television series? Every week, Peter Falk, as a Los Angeles homicide detective, solved a case with his eye for detail and strange interrogation techniques.

Columbo's real life problem would have been a lack of forensic evidence. Knowing who did it and *proving* who did it are two separate things. Prosecutors don't like losing and the quickest way to loose a homicide case is to show up without hard evidence.

The crime scene investigators on television are even further off than Columbo. Almost everything they do is *possible* — with the exception of seemingly instant DNA testing — but crime scene technicians do not run investigations — detectives do. The two jobs are specialized. Detectives don't do crime scene work these days and technicians don't do investigations.

Making an arrest and having it tossed for a lack of probable cause weakens the case against the real criminal when he or she is caught because it leaves the defense lawyers with ready-made doubt for the jury. Slow and steady is the best way to proceed with an investigation when it's possible to do so.

The first homicide I ever saw as a patrol officer was essentially solved ten minutes after I arrived on the scene. Two neighbors told me that the woman's brother-in-law did it because he and the dead woman had been having an affair she wanted to end.

They were right and the suspect admitted upfront that his hair and body fluid would be found in her bed because he had been there often. For two years, the homicide detective stayed at it, periodically calling in the suspect. When the homicide officer had enough to confront the suspect, the suspect said he wanted a lawyer, then went home and blew his head off with a shotgun.

Professor Jon Wyatt, Jed Osteen and Ron Oxendine were all viable suspects. All of them knew enough about Aztec warriors and sacrificial practices from Mesoamerica to have put together the scenario. Other than the murder weapons under Osteen's bed, that virtually screamed out "set-up," nothing connected them to the scene of the murder.

Not only diligence is required in investigations. Luck comes in handy.

These thoughts were on my mind as I wheeled into the sally port garage of the Sheriff's Office. A sallyport was once an opening in fortified buildings or castles, from which defenders could sally forth to meet the enemy. In jails and prisons, the sally port is the entrance and exit, usually with a double system of locks that have to be operated by separate keys from each side.

I had just parked my old maroon Ford and was locking up when corrections officers came running from all directions, pouring into the caged area where prisoners were taken down on an elevator. I stopped a young officer with a blond buzz cut. "What's going on?"

"Hostage situation in seven tank," he replied, then ran on.

Seven tank had been maximum security when the downtown facility had been the only jail. Now the old jail, circa 1979, is an intake center, but *all* the prisoners held there are maximum security. The baddest of the bad still live in seven tank. I had just put my pistol into the gun drawer and the corrections officer was locking it up when my old friend and boss, Sheriff Sam Renfro put his hand on my shoulder.

"Where might you be going, Shy?"

"There's a hostage situation and I'm a negotiator, Sam."

"Bullshit, Shy! You heard the word *hostage* and went into cop mode. This ain't 1980 and you ain't thirty years old any longer. We'll both go down but when it comes time to swarm the tank, we'll let those husky young guys do it. We clear?"

"Loud and clear, Boss. Come on, the elevator's ready to go."

We stepped onto the elevator and were assaulted by the odor of urine, flatulence, grease from the kitchen with a tinge of disinfectant. After a while, the people who work in the jail no longer notice it. We stepped off into a crowd of corrections officers, donning body armor and helmets with face guards.

"Remember when six of us used to run this jail at night, Sam?"

"This was where we all made our bones back then. All right, everyone listen up!" Sam raised his voice and the murmuring went silent. "Somebody report!"

A young sergeant stepped forward. "Sheriff, an inmate faked a seizure and Officer Matt Krieg went in to check. Officer Darnell Johnson stood by the door waiting on backup. When the inmates grabbed Krieg, Johnson locked it down. They've got some kind of homemade shank, holding it to Krieg's throat."

"What do they want, Sergeant Ivy?" Sam asked.

"We don't know yet, Sheriff."

"Tempest, walk down the back walk and see what their demands are," Sam said. "But stay out of range of the bars."

"Someone bring me a cup of coffee," I said

"What...?" the sergeant began.

"Get him coffee," Sam said. "He's going to look relaxed and in control when he goes back there."

"Get an entrance team ready," I said to the sergeant when he brought me a steaming cup of coffee. "If I drop this cup, send the team in."

Entrance to all the tanks or cellblocks are on the side opposite the day room, where prisoners spend most of their time. The officers who feed them and do the counts have no keys. As I walked onto the backwalk and turned left, it was as if time had rolled backwards and I was a rookie jailer again.

The inmates in nine tank and eight tank had been locked down in their cells. I stopped behind seven tank and saw that they had Officer Krieg sitting at one of the tables and benches, which are bolted to the floor. One inmate, a white male with a dirty blond ponytail stood behind him with something I could not see distinctly held to his throat. I stood sipping coffee until one of the inmates noticed me.

"Who the hell are you?" A black man with a shaved head asked. *The leader,* I decided.

"I'm assistant chief Shy Tempest, who the hell are *you*?"

He was a big one, maybe three hundred pounds and somewhat taken aback by my question. "I'm Yusef Mohammed, the man who will decide whether Officer Krieg here dies or not."

"Is that what you think, Yusef?"

"I don't think it, I *know* it!"

"Yusef, did you know that the day Officer Krieg came to work here he was told that in a case where he was taken hostage, the department would not negotiate his release?"

"That's bullshit! You ain't gonna stand here and let me cut his throat," he said.

"Ask Officer Krieg if he knew he was expendable when he started to work."

Yusef turned to Krieg, a stocky man of medium height. "They really tell you that, boy?"

Krieg nodded his head affirmatively. The young man was holding up better than most would have in the custody of killers, rapists and armed robbers.

"Then how come you ain't already stormed us," Yusef asked.

"Well," I took a sip of coffee, "we would rather you *didn't* kill one of our officers, but every officer knows the risk. I did two years, two days and four hours on this back walk in 1981 and 1982. If you have some kind of reasonable request or complaint, now's the time to tell me. If I walk away, it's all over but the crying."

"I want a car delivered to the front of the City-County buildin' on Hill Avenue. We're leavin' and takin' Officer Krieg with us. We'll turn him loose when we see nobody's followin'."

"Never going to happen in your lifetime, Yusef." I said, taking a sip of coffee.

"What the hell kinda hostage negotiator are you?" Yusef almost screamed. "You never say *no* to somebody with a hostage!"

"You saw that movie, too? Samuel L. Jackson starred in it, right? The thing is Yusef, you don't have a *civilian* hostage. You have a cop who already knew what would happen if he was taken hostage.

"You've got two, maybe three, people with you, Yusef. The rest of these inmates were not in on it and want no part in it. If we stand here long enough, even your buddies are going to get weak. The best possible ending is that you hand officer Krieg that shank and let him walk.

"The worst possible ending is if you hurt the officer or start to hurt the officer, there are several husky, young officers from the Special Operations Response Team, just itching to get their hands on you. I'm the only thing keeping them off you right now. Because they *want* you, Yusef." I took another sip of coffee.

Yusef unexpectedly raised the ante. "Suppose I show you the color of this boy's blood?"

Before I could say anything else, one of the inmates in the background charged the man holding the blade to Krieg's throat, grabbed his arm and jerked him away. I dropped the coffee cup and the SORT team officers with riot sticks, body armor and helmets with face guards, charged down the side walk and into the day room.

Most of the inmates flattened themselves against the bars, hands raised. Yusef might have been raising his hands, but he wasn't fast enough. One of the corrections officers using the riot stick like a bayoneted rifle, hit the big man in the groin with a vertical stroke, then swung the stick in a horizontal strike against the side of Yusef's head.

The inmate with the blond ponytail had stabbed the man who grabbed him several times before the correction officers could stop him.

Knees shaking and hands trembling, I walked back around and took a seat on one of the green benches outside the control room. In a moment, corrections officers came carrying the stabbed inmate down the hall and put him on the elevator to a waiting ambulance. He was covered in so much blood I couldn't see his face.

Then the Sheriff and Sergeant Ivy came around with Officer Krieg. He looked rattled, as well he should have been. "Krieg, sit down with Chief Tempest, I'm going to get us some coffee."

"Sheriff, *I'll* get the coffee," Sergeant Ivy said.

"Ivy, I was fetching coffee from that very kitchen before you were old enough to work here. You can come and help me carry it, though."

"Chief..." Krieg said, "I'm glad you were here today."

"Officer Krieg, you showed grace under pressure this morning, I just talked a little. I'm good with words."

"I've read your books, Chief. You *are* good with words."

"Talking's a lot easier, Officer Krieg, without a knife to your throat."

"Hell's bells," Sam Renfro, said coming from the kitchen. "I'd forgotten how bad the coffee is down here. "Let's go to my office for some *good* coffee. You too, Krieg. You need a break."

As we rode up on the elevator, I turned to Krieg. "Who was the inmate that got stabbed? It was a foolhardy move, but it took some *cojones*."

"His name's Jorge Chávez," Krieg said.

"*Jorge Chávez*?" I repeated.

"Yeah. He's a model prisoner. You know him, Chief?"

"I met him once, the day he tried to shoot me."

"That's incredible, Chief," Kreg said. "If he hadn't tried to shoot you, I might be dead."

It's a rare occasion when Jennifer gets home before I do. When I went through the kitchen door, I caught the poignant ginger-garlic odor of Asian cuisine and saw that Jen was setting the table. Magdala ran up, wiggling in canine delight and licked my hand as I stopped to pet her.

"I decided to whip up some takeout from Mandarin House before you got home," Jen said. "I got General Tso's chicken and hot and sour soup for you."

My lovely *compañera* came over and kissed me, eliciting a whimper of complaint from our German Shepherd. "You look tired. Rough day? Did it have something to do with the hostage situation this morning?"

"Yes and yes," I answered, pulling a chair from under the table and sitting down. "I was the negotiator."

Jennifer brought a cup of dark, rich coffee with one teaspoon of sugar and set it in front of me. "They said on the news that an inmate was stabbed but is in satisfactory condition. Do you know who it was?"

"It was Jorge Chávez," I said, taking a sip of coffee.

"He took part in the hostage situation?"

"In a manner of speaking. He was stabbed preventing the attempted murder of a corrections officer."

"Did you see him?" Jennifer asked.

"I was twenty feet away when he was stabbed, and I went by the hospital to check on him. He'll be free to do what he wants in a day or two."

"Well, maybe in light of the circumstances, the judge will lower the bond," she said.

"No, I said he'll be *free* in a day or two. I got him released from jail on his own recognizance and went to see the attorney general. I had the charge reduced to simple assault.

"If he goes to court and pleads guilty, he will get diversion for ninety days and the assault charge will be dismissed. He needs to understand that if he doesn't show up he'll never be eligible for citizenship because this will be hanging over his head."

Jennifer was quiet for a moment. Finally, she said: "That was very generous of you, Shiloh. I'll go see him in the hospital and tell him the good news."

"He *redeemed* himself this morning. What he did was stupid but brave. I didn't forgive him; I just had to acknowledge his redemption."

"Shiloh, as long as I live, I'll never understand men. You're all like little boys on the playground, strutting around. Whenever you compete, it always comes down to who has the bigger set of *cojones*.

"Then without warning, one of you will do something noble. I'm sure the attorney general didn't agree to this without argument."

"No, he didn't. Tomorrow, you can tell Jorge we're even and he'll never get a break like this again."

"I will make him understand that, Shiloh."

Sixteen

My department cell phone rang at seven the next morning. I don't like cell phones and I don't like pagers. I was the last detective to get a pager before the former sheriff put me out on disability and I never had a cell phone until I went back.

"Shy Tempest here."

"I wake you up, Chief?" Tom Abernathy asked.

"It's okay, Tom. I should have been out of here half an hour ago. What's up?" Jennifer had an early deposition and I had drifted off again after she left.

"Professor Jon Wyatt is coming in with his attorney this morning at nine. I thought you might want to be here."

"You're not worried about your chief?" I asked.

"No, my soon to be former partner was updating the chief every time we met with you. Hodge called me on the carpet and I told him every major break we've made came from you."

"Too bad about Claiborne," I said. "Still, it's better to know now than find out when something big is in the works."

"He told Hodge about me dumping the powder we found in Jerry's apartment. I denied it and said you'd back me up, so the chief decided not to make an issue of it." Abernathy said.

"Not just a social climber, then, but a real cheese-eater, that Claiborne."

"He's going to work for internal affairs, after a few vacation days. You and I are working this case alone now."

"All right, Tom. I'll be there by nine."

As I was getting ready to leave, an old saying came to me: "A friend is somebody who knows where the bodies are buried, but a *real* friend is the one who helped you bury them." It's an exaggeration, of course, but there's a basic police truism hidden there. If you can't trust your partner, there's *nobody* you can trust.

In the kitchen, I put out fresh food and water for Magdala, then went outside with her so she could relieve herself, have a run and check the perimeter of the yard. As I watched her trot around I knew that to her sensitive nose, volumes had been written about raccoons, squirrels and, probably, coyotes during the night.

A trainer once told me that to a German Shepherd's sensitive sense of smell, a set of footprints in the grass from the night before is as distinct as a newly-mowed lawn to the human nose. It made me wonder how dogs tolerate people and their perfumes and colognes.

When I called Magdala, she reluctantly returned to the house and went inside. "Be good Magdala," I said as I was leaving. "Guard the house."

She laid down with a sigh. Placing her long snout on her paws, she made one final attempt to make me feel guilty about leaving her by fixing her eloquent gaze on me.

The traffic was still heavy when I headed downtown to the safety building. I made a conscious effort to relax and lit a Camel filtered cigarette, one of my few remaining vices. I saw a bumper sticker on the car ahead of me that said: "Jesus is coming soon," then in smaller letters, "And boy is he pissed!" There are people with a sense of humor, even here on the buckle of the Bible Belt.

As I pulled into the parking lot of the safety building, which houses city court, I saw Jon Wyatt's green Austin Healey Sprite. The Knoxville Police Department once had a functioning jail, and since it was too early for court, the large parking lot was mostly empty.

In the lobby, I flashed my star and the officer in the control room waved and punched a button to summon the elevator. A couple of minutes later, I stepped off the elevator into the criminal investigation section where we had interviewed the professor before. I saw that Wyatt and a man I presumed to be his attorney were sitting at the desk with Tom Abernathy.

"Pull up a seat, Chief," Abernathy said. "You know Professor

Wyatt and this is his attorney, Lawrence Birdwell. The lawyer rose and shook my hand but Wyatt very pointedly did not. I pulled up a spare chair.

"Gentlemen," Birdwell said, "I'd like to go on record by pointing out that Professor Wyatt is here voluntarily." The name fit Birdwell. He was thin, fortyish, and moved jerkily as he used his hands and head to gesture. I could imagine him pecking the food off of a plate,

"So noted, Mister Birdwell," Abernathy said.

"Professor Wyatt will require immunity for a portion of what he has to say in order to prove his whereabouts the night Jerry Carpenter was killed."

"I can't grant immunity, Mister Birdwell, that's a decision to be made by the attorney general. You should know that. However, if the professor wasn't committing a felony when he did whatever it was he was doing, we have absolutely no interest. We're working a murder."

"*Immunity* was a poor choice of words," Birdwell said, obviously embarrassed at having been corrected on a point of law by a mere police officer. "What Professor Wyatt was doing wasn't felonious, but it would be extremely embarrassing if his colleagues and employer found out about it. We would expect discretion on your part."

"We're nothing if not discrete," Abernathy said. "All we want to do is clear Professor Wyatt as a suspect so that we don't have to waste any more time. If he can prove he was somewhere else when Jerry Carpenter was killed, and wasn't committing a felony, he can trust our discretion."

"All right," Birdwell nodded to his client, "show it to them."

Wyatt took out his wallet and removed what appeared to be a credit card receipt and handed it to Abernathy, who read it, then passed it to me. It was a credit card receipt for a cheap motel in East Knox County. It was dated for the evening of Jerry Carpenter's death.

"That should clear things up," Birdwell said.

"Not by itself," I said. "This only proves that you rented a room that evening, Jon. Even if the clerk remembers you, it still doesn't prove you didn't leave there and kill Jerry. You have to do better than this."

"What do you want me to do, produce the person I was with?" Wyatt asked.

"That's exactly what you have to do, Professor," Abernathy responded.

"If I did *that*... well, it's just ludicrous," Wyatt said.

"Jon, for a man with a doctorate in anthropology," I said, "you're remarkably dense about the way the world works. If you give us what we need, you lose access to a prostitute and maybe her pimp, but you won't have suspicion of murder hanging over your head any longer. Wake up, here!"

"He's right, Professor," Birdwell said.

"I really don't want strangers discussing my sex life with *anyone*," Wyatt's voice was tinged with desperation. Besides, I don't even *know* her real name. She just goes by Brandi."

"Jon, how do you contact her?" I asked.

"I don't... there's a go-between..."

"Her pimp?" Abernathy said.

"She calls him her *business manager*," Wyatt said angrily.

"You say toe-*mah*-to and I say toe-*may*-to," Abernathy said. "Call him and tell him to have Brandi meet you at the same place as last time, at three this afternoon."

"You mean call him right now?" Wyatt asked.

"Right now, Jon. And we're getting tired of playing games," I said. "And don't arouse his suspicion. Do it the same way you always do. Make it happen. If you don't, we'll show up and question you at the next faculty meeting."

Professor Wyatt, red in the face, took out his cell phone and punched in one number. He apparently had the pimp on speed dial. A moment later he said: "Yes, this is Mister Wiggins. I would like to meet Brandi at three this afternoon."

He listened a moment, then said: "No, I wouldn't be interested in another girl."

Wyatt's face reddened slightly, "All right, if that's what it will take, I'll pay it."

He closed the phone and glanced at us. "He says it's Brandi's day off and it will cost double her usual rate."

"Just out of curiosity, what's Brandi's regular rate?" Abernathy asked.

"Five hundred dollars for an all-nighter," Wyatt said.

"How does she know which room?" I asked.

"It's the same room every time, unless he tells me something different. It's room 307," Wyatt said. "It will be unlocked. The desk clerk is in on it."

"When may we be hearing from you?" Birdwell asked.

"If the professor's story checks out, I'll be in touch this afternoon. You two know the way out," Abernathy said.

When they were gone, Abernathy turned to me. "You ever hire a pro, Shy?"

"Once, while I was at Fort Jackson, South Carolina during the Vietnam War. A group of us went to a place in Columbia called the Chicken Nook. I paid for the room and the girl came in. Beautiful, young black woman.

"When I actually was faced with the prospect of paying for something so intimate, I gave her the money and told her to take a break. That was my first and last experience with a prostitute — until I worked organized crime."

"It's a pretty disgusting business," Abernathy said. "I had a similar experience once."

"You up for lunch, Tom?" I didn't really want to hear his story.

"Sure, what do you have in mind, Chief?"

"How about Bojangles?" I said.

"You're a cheap date, Chief. But Bojangles is fine with me."

Abernathy and I had borrowed a car from the narcotic officers so we wouldn't stick out like a sore thumb when we pulled into what had once been part of a successful chain of motels but was now a combination rent-by-the-hour facility and flophouse. There was nobody in sight as we entered the unlocked door and locked it behind us.

Probably without conscious thought, Abernathy made sure the room was clear by opening the closet and then pushing back the shower curtain in the bathroom. Cops fear surprise attacks the way small mammals fear attack from above.

"This place is a dump, Chief."

"Tell me about it. This is the kind of place where you find empty condom packs when you turn back the sheets."

"She should be here any minute," Abernathy said. "When she knocks, I'll go in the bathroom and close the door. She's expecting a white college professor and I don't want to present her with a large black man and have her bolt on us."

"It's possible she'll try to bolt when she sees me. But you're right. There's no use in going out of our way to spook her."

I lit a cigarette and settled in the room's single chair while Abernathy sat on the bed, fishing out a cigarette of his own.

"You ever thought about giving up smoking?" Abernathy asked.

"Why do you ask, Tom?"

"I was just curious, with your heart and all."

"One day it will stop and I'll probably be smoking when it does."

A tiny knock echoed through the room. Abernathy walked quietly to the bathroom and shut the door. I waited until he was out of sight before I opened it.

Brandi turned out to be a small woman of perhaps twenty-five. She was not particularly pretty by my standards, with hair bleached platinum and heavily made up, but I could see how she would appeal to some men.

She stared a me for a second but did not panic as she spoke. "Where's Wiggins?"

"Taking a leak," I replied.

She hesitated only a moment then stepped through the door. "It's going to cost extra for two of you."

"Not a problem," I replied, shutting the door and putting on the chain.

When Abernathy walked out of the bathroom, Brandi still didn't panic. "Whatever is going on here, let's get the transaction out of the way before we start."

"Yes, let's do that," I said. Both of us flashed our badges.

"You're not vice," she said. "I know all of them."

"You're right, we're homicide, but we can still take you to jail and see that it's tomorrow before you make bail," I told her.

Brandi sat down on the bed and fished a pack of thin, feminine cigarettes from her purse. She lit one and took a deep drag. "Okay, what do you want."

"We need to know when was the last time you saw Wiggins. The *exact* time and date," I told her.

She took out an expensive PDA and began to punch numbers. Somehow it didn't surprise me that a call girl had her own personal handheld computer. When she was finished, she handed it to me. The calendar note with a date on it said, "Mr. Wiggins, aka Jon Wyatt" had been with her from seven the night Jerry Carpenter was killed until eight the next morning.

"Jon would be shocked to know that you have his real name," I said, handing the PDA to Abernathy.

"My business manager is very clever," Brandi said. "He keeps up with technology and I knew Jon Wyatt's real name and address before I met him the first time. Is that all you wanted from me?"

"That's it," Abernathy said, "you've cleared the professor."

"Since I have some time on my hands," Brandi said, "I wouldn't mind banking a little good will."

"You already have, Brandi," I told her. "I hope your *business manager* doesn't consider taking action against Jon Wyatt. He really had no choice but to give you up — and we'll be watching."

"No harm, no foul," she said, putting out her cigarette. "Going after a whitebread customer would be bad for business. Are you finished with me?"

"Bye bye, Brandi." I said.

"Color me gone," she said. "This appointment has already cost me a lot of money."

Brandi got up, put the PDA in her purse and left.

Seventeen

Magdala trotted beside me on the walking path at Fountain City Park on Broadway. Owned by the Lion's Club, it has been a fixture in North Knoxville for as long as I remember. I got my first kiss under one of the large oak trees, as well as my second. School and church wiener roasts were a big social item for junior high school kids when I was young.

"Oh, what a beautiful dog!" A thirtyish woman in tight white shorts and a tank top stopped to pet Magdala, who took it all in stride, standing patiently. "Is she a full-blooded German Shepherd?" the woman asked.

"She sure is," I answered, as the woman resumed her speed walk around the park and I enjoyed the view. The woman was in good shape.

As we got to the little spring that trickles over rocks and empties into a larger stream, Magdala pulled on her leash and I followed her to the edge of the water where she got a drink. There were a few children swinging and a couple with a toddler were letting him use the slide, but there were no picnics in progress under any of the sheds.

While Magdala was lapping the water, my cell phone rang. "Tempest, talk to me."

"Chief, this is Abernathy. I called your office and they said you were off."

"Took a personal day," I told him. "What's up?"

"Can I meet you somewhere?" he asked.

"I'm at Fountain City Park walking Magdala," I told him.

"I'm on I-75 at Merchants. I'll get off and come down Cedar Lane," he said.

"We'll be on a bench on the street side of the park," I told him.

Magdala and I resumed our walk and by the time I arrived at the bench, I saw Abernathy's unmarked Ford slow down as he looked for a parking space along the street. "Let's take a break, Magdala." Her ears went up and she cocked her head to look at me. But when I sat down, so did she.

As Abernathy strolled towards us, carrying a large evidence envelope, Magdala went in full alert and a low rumble came from her chest. "It's all right, Magdala," I told her. She visibly relaxed and watched Abernathy approach with curiosity, but no aggression.

"I don't think I would want to approach you without her permission," Abernathy said.

"She is very protective," I said. "Have a seat."

"Is that the dog you rescued from the thug?"

"One and the same," I said.

"She looks like the genuine article."

"That she is, Tom. A much better pedigree than I have."

"I got DNA evidence back on the cigarette butts and fake fingernail."

"Since you're not jumping up and down, I take it that it didn't solve the case," I said.

"The two butts had DNA from the same male subject, but there just wasn't enough fingernail left to extract DNA," he said.

"The male isn't in the database, I take it."

"No. The only way it will help us is if we find a suspect to match."

"That's why they call it an investigation," I said.

"You don't seem too concerned, Chief."

"I never made a case with DNA until I came back after a long time away. The science was still in its infancy when I left. I suppose I just don't put as much credence on it as you kiddies do."

"Where do we go from here, Chief?"

"Back to square one. Well, not all the way back, we still need to interview Oxendine," I said.

"That reminds me," Abernathy reached into the brown evidence envelope to bring out what looked like a business letter. "Here's the comparison between Jerry Carpenter and Ron Oxendine. I didn't open it, since it was for you."

"I don't think I'll open it either," I said. "I'm going to let Oxendine open it himself. Maybe I can leverage him a little bit."

"When are you going back to work, Chief?"

"Probably tomorrow," I said.

"Would you like to take this evidence with you and look at it when you have time?" Abernathy asked.

"Sure, if it won't cause you problems," I said.

"The only problem I have right now is that we still don't know who killed Jerry Carpenter. I'll worry about my chief later."

"I like your attitude, Investigator Abernathy."

Jennifer and I were in our sunroom, sitting in twin recliners and enjoying our evening coffee. I had carried in the envelope with the Jerry Carpenter evidence and was considering going through it. Jen was reading a novel and Magdala was taking a nap beside my chair.

"Is that a romance novel?" I asked.

"I'm escaping for a little while," she answered, looking up and smiling, "what else would it be?"

"Is it about a poor but virtuous young woman secretly in love with a wealthy man way above her social circle or is it about a rich girl in love with a penniless but passionately ethical young man?"

"It's more the latter," she answered. "But romances have changed from the old bodice rippers. There's even a slot for *your* genre now."

"Not for me. Romance writers work way too hard. Besides, you know I'm joking. Some of my best friends are romance writers — and they cover the spectrum from suspense romances to science fiction. A romance is no easier to write than anything else."

"I *do* know that, but you throw me a curve every time you seem to be describing the plot of something I'm reading," Jennifer said.

"You know my guiding principle, Jen. There are only three plots with infinite variations: The individual in conflict with another individual; the individual in conflict with God or nature; and the individual in conflict with him or herself."

"So you say, Shiloh. May I read my book in silence, please?"

"If you wish," I said, opening the large evidence envelope.

I put the results of Ron Oxendine's comparison with Jerry Carpenter on the table beside me and went over the results from the two cigarette butts found at the scene. Then I read the report on the fake fingernail that was listed as "artificial nail, green, with small nail fragment attached. Results inconclusive for DNA due to insufficient sample."

"Son of a bitch," I said aloud.

"What?" Jennifer said somewhat impatiently.

"Nothing," I told her. *A green artificial fingernail. The evidence had been there all along but I hadn't seen it before it went to the lab and I hadn't asked about the color.*

"Magdala, let's go for a walk," I said. The big German Shepherd jumped up and ran to the kitchen where she would be waiting beside the leash hanging next to the door.

"Be sure and take a flashlight," Jennifer said. "I thought you had already taken her out for a walk."

"I did, but this one's for me. I have some nervous energy to expend. It's too late to get Abernathy up and I think I just solved Jerry Carpenter's murder."

"Be careful," Jennifer said. She had been with me way too long to pay any attention to my fevered rantings.

Eighteen

It was one of those East Tennessee mornings when everything comes together perfectly. Blue skies with fluffy clouds drifting down to touch the surrounding mountains and a temperature in the low seventies.

Though Appalachian born and bred, I have never lived in the mountains, I live *between* mountains in the Tennessee Valley. There's a difference outsiders wouldn't recognize between living on and living between mountains. I've never been comfortable anywhere the land is flat — especially on the coasts near oceans.

I had a breakfast appointment with Tom Abernathy. I had managed to contain my excitement. He had no idea of the energy bubbling in me. As far as he knew, I just wanted company for breakfast. The cell phone startled me slightly when it went off. I fished it out of my jacket pocket. "Tempest here, go ahead."

"Good morning, Chief Tempest."

"Good morning, Ron. I was wondering when you would be checking in."

"Just called to see if you had any results from my DNA comparison yet?"

"That I do, Ron. That I do."

"And?" he said.

"I haven't opened the letter from the lab yet," I said.

"When *will* you open the results?" he inquired.

"I'm not going to open the envelope. When you come in to talk to me, *you* can open it," I told him.

"That was not part of the agreement, Chief."

"An agreement made while one person is holding a gun on another person wouldn't be valid, anyway, Ron. I did what I said I would do."

"I can't argue with that," he said.

"Why don't you come in and let us clear you, Ron?"

"Not until you arrest the person who murdered Jerry, Chief. I just don't trust anybody with a sword hanging over my head. No offense. Besides, I thought you would have solved the case by now. You got my DNA back, so you should have the rest of the evidence too."

"What are you getting at, Jerry?"

"*Cherchez la femme,* Chief. You're the detective. Find the woman Jerry was with the night he was murdered and you'll have the killer."

"Are you suggesting Professor Clark was involved?"

"You know damned well who I'm talking about and it wasn't Deborah Clark *that* night!" he said.

"Ron, it sounds as if you may have the information we need to break this case."

"You break the case and I'll add my testimony, but there are too many innocent men doing time because it was easier to make a case against them than to keep on investigating. Later, Chief Tempest." The line went dead.

I pondered what he had said for the rest of my trip to Rankin Restaurant on Central. Tom Abernathy was flirting with the waitress when I arrived and she was flirting back. Apparently she saw the resemblance to Denzel Washington. Or maybe Abernathy was handsome. Heterosexual men don't have the inclination or data to judge beauty in other men.

"Nothing sadder than a cop eating breakfast alone," I said. "Breakfast is on me. Eat hearty, Tom. I have good news."

"All right, in that case, I'll have three eggs over easy *and* sausage and biscuits," he told the waitress.

"I'll have the same," I told the waitress, "but I'll need low cholesterol eggs."

The young woman stared at me like a rabbit caught in the headlights of a car until Abernathy rescued her. "He's just kidding, Mitzi. Bring the same thing for both of us."

She wrote down our orders, poured me a cup of coffee from

the pot she had carried to the table, then left, tossing me a nasty look.

"Chief, never tease a woman with a pot of scalding coffee in her hand. Didn't I mention that once before?"

"You'd think I'd know that by my age," I said.

"What are we celebrating, Chief?"

I took out the test sheet on the green fake fingernail nail from the evidence envelope and laid it on the table. Abernathy stared at it and shrugged.

"There wasn't enough real fingernail to test."

"True, but I know a woman who was wearing fake green fingernails the day after Jerry was killed and she and Jerry were lovers."

"Who?" Abernathy asked.

"Sadie Hyde, also known as Stormy in her profession as a nude dancer."

"I thought you had already discounted her? And why are you just now bringing it up?" Abernathy asked.

"That goes to show that you can't discount anyone. I didn't know the fake fingernail was green until I read the report. I never saw it."

"Damn," Abernathy said. "It slipped through the cracks because I didn't mention the color."

"And because *I* didn't ask, Tom. Don't try to hog all the stuff that goes wrong. If I had taken you to meet Sadie, you would have probably noticed the green nails." I took a sip of coffee and realized I had forgotten the sugar.

"So what's the plan?" Abernathy said.

"You need to get a court order signed for Sadie's cell phone records. I'm betting she called the big bouncer named Ralph Ogg at Sammy's place to help her finish off Jerry after she clubbed him unconscious. Then one of them drove Jerry's truck home while the other followed."

"Chief, you actually think a woman who earns her money getting naked is familiar with Aztec sacrifices. It sounds like a stretch," Abernathy said.

"Sadie is not stupid and Jed Osteen told us she was listening closely when he and Jerry were discussing the subject. I don't think she did the knife work, but Ralph Ogg is a big, strong boy and I'm hoping the DNA on the cigarette butts belongs to him.

"We know Jed Osteen never locks his door. Sadie knew where he lived because she had been there. All she had to do was carry the weapons in and put them under the bed."

"Sounds logical," Abernathy said.

"I think Ron Oxendine can put Jerry and Sadie together the night of the murder."

"How so?" Abernathy said.

"He called this morning on his throwaway cell phone, trying to find out the results of his DNA comparison with Jerry. I told him he'd have to take it out of my hand. Something he said leads me to believe he might have been at Sammy's Place that night. But he says he's not coming in until we arrest the murderer."

"Chief, I don't think it's wise to play games with Oxendine. I'm still not convinced we shouldn't have charged him with aggravated assault for holding us at gunpoint. I know you have a soft spot for war vets, but he's a dangerous man."

"I'll be careful, Tom."

"Claiborne and I were being careful the night he disarmed *us*. That boy has been places where none of us have ever been."

"One thing at a time, Tom. Sadie goes to work at three in the afternoon."

"Okay, Chief. I'll get the judge on the line for the court order and we'll pick her up today," Abernathy said.

"Good. I need to make an appearance at the sheriff's office this morning. I do draw a salary from there."

"That's mighty white of you, Chief," Tom said with a sly smile.

"Watch it, Officer. I'd hate to have to file charges against you for racial harassment. We white people are very sensitive, you know."

As I finished speaking, our food arrived and we dug in. When

I left, I picked up the check and left a hefty tip for the offended waitress in the name of future good will.

I paused respectfully in front of the sheriff's secretary because she was the keeper of the keys. She was busily flipping through a sheaf of papers. Finally, she looked up. "Chief, I've never met a man who can keep a simple checkbook, let alone run a multimillion dollar department."

"I can't disagree with that, Madeline," I said.

"*Can't* or have better sense, Chief?" She smiled. "Do you need to see Sam?"

"If he's not busy," I said.

"He's busy staying out of my way right now. He has a budget hearing tomorrow and didn't tell me until this morning. I'm spending my day catching up. Go on in, he needs the company." She punched the button and Sam's door unlocked.

Sam Renfro was wearing a blue seersucker suit with a light blue shirt and a blue and white striped tie. He had been dressing the part of a stylish Southern gentleman since being appointed sheriff after his former boss was indicted for bribery. In our days in narcotics, nobody looked grungier than Sam.

"You look like Andy Griffith as *Matlock* in that suit," I said.

"Shiloh, don't come in here and treat me disrespectfully while I'm hiding from my secretary. I *am* the Sheriff."

"Yeah, I bet you don't spring another budget hearing on her without warning," I said.

"She told you, huh? Want some coffee, Shy?"

"Sure," I said.

He poured a cup of coffee into one of his blue and gold cups with the department's seven pointed star on it, dropped in one lump of sugar and handed it across the desk.

"Is this one of those meetings where I'm going to need a cigarette?" Sam asked.

"It can be, if you like," I replied.

He opened a desk drawer and brought out the old metal ashtray and a butane lighter. He only smokes on occasion and only with me. Since I came back to work he needs a cigarette now and then to calm his nerves.

I shook a Camel filter out of my pack. Sam took it, lit it and leaned back in the pretentious expensive leather chair the previous sheriff had bought. Sam had taken out all the elaborate paintings and the only thing on his desk was a picture of his father, a former KPD chief.

"Are you here to tell me you're going to stay on as chief of detectives?" Sam asked, blowing a smoke ring.

"How much time do I have left, Sam, before I have to decide?"

"If we didn't go back so far, you'd have run out of time already. Hell, if you don't want to be chief of detectives, be my chief deputy. I inherited him."

"I'm more likely to stay as chief of dicks. Chief deputy is mostly public relations, Sam." I said, shaking out a cigarette and lighting it.

"Well, you could think of it as public service. The good of the many and all that, Shy."

"Yeah, until the first time I told a county commissioner to shove it up his ass, it might work."

"You have a point there, Shy. For a man of words, you're pretty blunt." He blew another smoke ring, then put his finger through it. "Next Thursday you hit the maximum you can make and stay on retirement. I'd keep you on as a consultant forever, but the retirement board wouldn't stand for it."

"I'll let you know Monday, Sam."

"Good, because your friend Al Reagan isn't going to put in a bid for lieutenant until he knows you're going to be his boss. You should have lieutenants you trust."

Nineteen

There were only two cars on the lot of Sammy's Place when Abernathy and I pulled in, a new red Mercedes roadster and an old Buick, circa 1970.

"I see they get a diverse clientele here," Abernathy said.

"These strip joints always have attracted a wide range of men," I replied.

We locked my maroon Ford and walked across the parking lot, gravel crunching beneath our feet. As we entered the foyer, I saw Sammy himself was on the door. He punched the button and unlocked the inner door, without speaking.

We stepped into the bar and paused long enough to allow our eyes to adjust to the low light inside. I heard Sammy sigh deeply.

"Chief, I've watched you walk into my bar for more than twenty years now. I can tell you didn't just come for information today," Sammy said, pushing his white hair back from his forehead. It was a nervous gesture I had seen many times.

"Sammy, this is Tom Abernathy, a KPD investigator. We need to see Sadie," I said.

"She's in the dressing room. Do I need to call in a replacement for Sadie."

"I'm afraid so, Sammy," I said. "Where's the oversized thug who usually sits on the door?"

"He ain't here yet," Sammy said. "Usually gets here between three and four in the afternoon. You takin' him, too, Shy."

"No," I replied, disingenuously, because I didn't want the big man to bolt. "When he gets here, don't mention that we're talking to Sadie."

"You know where she is," Sammy said, obviously not committing to keeping our presence a secret.

We walked to the back, past the bartender and another dancer standing at the bar. I opened the door to the makeshift dressing room and Abernathy and I entered. Sadie was sitting at the dressing table in a black lace bra and panties. She glanced at us, then went on applying mascara.

"If it isn't Chief of Detectives Shy Tempest and the Denzel Washington clone from KPD. How can I help you, gentlemen?" she said.

"You can pull on some street clothes, Sadie. You're under arrest," I said.

A tremor passed through her body, but she recovered quickly. "What am I being arrested for?" she asked.

"The murder of Jerry Carpenter," Abernathy said. "You have the right to remain silent and the right to the presence of an attorney..."

"I *know* my rights!" Sadie snapped.

"However," Abernathy went on as if he hadn't been interrupted, "even if you choose to speak to us without an attorney, you have the right to stop speaking at any time and request an attorney. Do you understand your rights?"

"I just *told* you I understand them," Sadie said, "and I've already told Shy Tempest that I ain't got no knowledge of what happened to Jerry."

"Put on your street clothes, Sadie," I told her.

Glaring at us, Sadie pulled on a pair of tight-fitting jeans, slipped her feet into a pair of sandals and pulled a yellow knit blouse over her head. She picked up her pocketbook, but Abernathy took it from her hand.

"Sadie, turn around and put your hands behind your back. We'll take care of your purse," he said.

As Abernathy cuffed her, I opened the purse and found the cell phone I had expected and a small, cheap Raven .25 caliber pistol, with some kind of gold-tone finish and pink grips. "Gun, partner," I said.

"You call that a gun, Chief Tempest?" Sadie said contemptuously. "A friend of mine gave it to me years ago when the company was advertising it as a *lady's* gun. I've never even fired it."

"Sadie, you must consider it to be a weapon, otherwise why carry it?" I asked.

As we led Sadie out of the dressing room. The lone dancer at the bar and the bartender stared, seeming to show only mild interest.

"Sammy, it looks like Tiny is running late," I said.

"No, he pulled in, saw your car and took off like a bat out of hell," Sammy said.

"The wicked flee when no man pursues," I said.

Sadie was silent on the way to jail. We had decided to take her to my office because she would be booked at the City-County building after we interrogated her. Besides, we wanted to avoid running into Abernathy's chief, Frank Hodge.

We pulled into my reserved parking space at the sheriff's department sally port, walked to the central elevators and dropped down to level one where criminal investigations was housed. Originally, the sheriff's office had been in one section but the department had grown since 1979 when the City-County building opened.

We led Sadie to my office and took off the handcuffs. She rubbed her wrists where the cuffs had pressed down on the flesh.

"Have a seat, Sadie," I said.

Abernathy closed my office door and sat down beside Sadie across from my desk. He put a Miranda warning and a ballpoint pen in front of her and said. "I need you to sign right here that you understand your rights, Sadie."

"Why should I do anything you ask?" Sadie said.

"Well, if you don't, we're going to book you," I said. "Since we can't talk to you without an attorney if you don't sign, it's the only other choice we have. If we do that, you will sit in jail until your trial, next year some time."

"What about *probable cause*? I don't know much, but I watch television," she said.

I picked up the folder Abernathy had brought in earlier. "Sadie, we have your cell phone records. Sign the sheet, or not. But if you want to tell your side of the story, this is your last chance."

Sadie's face went pale and she picked up the pen and signed the Miranda waiver. "All right, ask your questions," she said.

"Why did you tell me you hadn't seen Jerry for three or four days before he was killed?" I asked.

"Because it's true," she said.

"Sadie, we have an eyewitness that puts Jerry at Sammy's Place the night somebody hit him in the head, then gutted him." Oxendine hadn't actually *said* it, but he implied that Jerry had been there that night.

"Maybe he *did* come in. On nights when I was really busy, we wouldn't even get a chance to talk. He'd just leave if I was really busy."

"Come on, Sadie," Abernathy said, "Sammy's Place is too small for you not to have noticed a friend and lover."

"You don't know how busy it gets," Sadie said.

"All right, Sadie, stick to your story. But please explain why your cell phone bounced a call off the tower nearest the World's Fair site to Sammy's Place in the early morning hours before Jerry's body was found."

"I'm a night person and so are all my friends. Maybe we went downtown looking for food. We do that a lot after work."

"After you made a call from near the World's Fair site to Sammy's Place, you got two cell phone calls from somebody who started in North Knox County and drove to the same area you called from, Sadie. We think it was Ralph Ogg and it won't be much trouble to look at *his* phone records if we have to."

"I think maybe Tiny and I *did* meet for burgers at Krystal on Cumberland Avenue that night, or rather early in the morning," Sadie said.

"So you drove past the Krystal on Clinton Highway, just a couple of miles from Sammy's Place, to eat at the Krystal on Cumberland where they serve the exact same food?" Abernathy said.

"Yes, it's comin' back now. That's what we did,' Sadie said. "We liked the atmosphere better."

"Then, after the two of you ate, you talked back and forth on your cell phones from downtown to North Knox County — in the vicinity of Jerry's apartment. That right?" Abernathy asked.

"It's been a while," she said. "But that sounds right." Sadie seemed to be growing more confident by the moment, which was what we had planned.

"Want to hear what we think happened, Sadie?" Abernathy asked.

Sadie looked at him and shrugged.

"We think Jerry drove you downtown to the World's Fair site, where the two of you had some kind of argument. You hit Jerry with the Aztec weapon he got from Jed Osteen. It didn't kill him, so you called Sammy's Place and Ralph Ogg came to your rescue. Then *he* gutted Jerry and the two of you drove Jerry's old pickup truck back to Jerry's place and parked it.

"Leaving the two Aztec weapons at Jed Osteen's house was no problem because you knew he never locked his house. How close are we, Sadie?"

"It doesn't matter what you *think*, does it?" Sadie snapped. "It's what you can *prove*, and you can't put me there because I *wasn't* there."

"Sadie, Sadie," I said, tossing the clear evidence bag with a fake, green fingernail on my desk, right in front of her. "Didn't you know that DNA could be extracted from what was left of your real nail when you broke off the fake one right next to the Sunsphere?"

When Sadie saw the fake fingernail, it was as if she shrank two sizes right in front of our eyes; her shoulders slumped and her face went pale.

"Sadie, it's time for the truth. You didn't kill Jerry, you just stunned him. Ogg killed him. You come clean and we can put most of this on him," I said.

"*Neither* of us killed him," Sadie said, with tears beginning to overflow her eyes and make streaks in her heavy makeup.

"Come on, Sadie. Ogg smoked two cigarettes at the foot of the Sunsphere. When we match his DNA to those cigarette butts, do you think he's going to go down alone?"

"We didn't kill him," Sadie said, shaking her head.

"Do you deny Ogg was there?" Abernathy asked.

"No," she said.

"Sadie, why don't you give us your side of the story," I said. She had no way of knowing that we *couldn't* extract her DNA from the fingernail. All we needed was her confession that she was there. Participation made both of them murderers under Tennessee law.

"Do you have a Kleenex?" Sadie asked.

Abernathy handed her a clean handkerchief from his pocket. She wiped her eyes and blew her nose. We waited while she collected her thoughts.

"Jerry showed up at Sammy's Place about midnight," she said. "He was drunk and stoned on painkillers and he tried to bring in those weapons that Jed had given him."

"Why would he have done that, Sadie?" I asked.

"Who knows *why* Jerry ever did *anything*? I guess he wanted to show them off. Tiny wouldn't let him in with the weapons and Jerry made a big scene. I went outside to talk him down. He said he'd leave if I'd go with him. It was a slow night, so I agreed because I didn't want Tiny to hurt Jerry, and I knew he *would* if he had to."

"What about the Aztec weapons, Sadie?" I asked.

"Jerry put them in his truck and told me he wanted to go watch the Sun come up over the Sunsphere, like a *real* Aztec warrior. I drove because he was too drunk." Sadie said.

"Where do you think *that* came from, Sadie?" I quietly asked, fascinated with what she thought she could make us believe.

"I *know* where that came from," she said. "He and Jed Osteen were joking about it when we were at Osteen's house. They were both wasted and talking about how the Sunsphere would have looked to an Aztec warrior somehow brought through time and dropped on the World's Fair site. I guess it just stuck in Jerry's mind. He already was playing with the weapons that night when he got to Sammy's Place."

"This sounds like a lot of desperate crap," Abernathy said.

"Let her tell the story," I said, reinforcing my role as the "good cop."

"By the time we got there, Jerry had settled down a little. But he got the knife and that club with the sharp edges out of the truck. We stepped over the orange nets the construction crew had put up and sat on the steps of the Sunsphere to wait for sunrise.

"That's when Jerry started talking about *her*," Sadie said.

"*Who* was he talking about, Sadie?" I asked quietly.

"Deborah Carter, his high school sweetheart," Sadie said, "the woman who slept in his bed on Thursday nights."

"Go on," I told her.

"He said Deborah wanted to make a life with him and he was *considering* it. I guess I went a little crazy myself when he said that." She wiped at her eyes again with the white handkerchief.

"Sadie, you told me you had no hope of ever having anything permanent with Jerry. You led me to believe that your relationship was more like friends with benefits than anything else," I said.

"I never *had* expected anything of Jerry that he couldn't give, but he was talking about making a life with another woman to *me,* like I was a piece of trash he'd picked up.

"I had nursed him through drunken bouts, hangovers and throwing up all over the place and he was talking about a life with *another* woman! Do you know how that made me feel?" Sadie sobbed out the last sentence.

"I imagine it made you feel pretty bad, Sadie," I said. "Was that when it happened?"

"Yes, I started screaming at Jerry and he did what he always did when we argued. He turned his back on me, put his hands over his ears and started walking towards the lake.

"That sword thing was leaning against the metal stairs and I picked it up and hit him." Sadie sobbed. "At first, I thought I had killed him. That's when I called Tiny to come and get me. Then Jerry made a noise and I saw he was still alive."

"Why didn't you use your cell to call for an ambulance, Sadie?" I asked.

"I was *scared.* When Tiny got there, he checked Jerry and said he was just out cold. We decided to leave him there and let him wake up on his own. He was always passing out in strange places. I just wanted to get away. I figured he wouldn't remember anything that happened and I'd just let on like we never had the conversation about Deborah Carter. I have some pride, you know," Sadie said. "I'm not *trash.*

"That's why it shocked me when you came to the club and told me that Jerry was dead. I figured he had woke up and called a cab and was at home sleepin' it off."

"Sadie, what about the charcoal grill, the little hibachi. Did you and Jerry take it, or did you tell Tiny to bring it."

"I don't know anything about a charcoal grill," she said.

"That's quite a story, Sadie," Abernathy said. "I suppose you think Tiny Ogg will tell us the same thing when we find him?"

"Tiny's not smart enough to lie," Sadie said. "Can I go back to work?"

"Not anytime soon, Sadie," Abernathy said.

"Chief Tempest, *you* believe me don't you?" she said. "You *know* I loved Jerry."

"It's quite a story, Sadie. But until we catch Tiny and hear what he has to say, you have to stay with us."

She sobbed quietly as Abernathy put the handcuffs back on her and led her off to the booking area. After they were gone, I called a friend of mine at a television station and a news crew was waiting when Abernathy came out of the jail after booking Sadie. His statement was short and concise.

TWENTY

Magdala met me at the kitchen door and I let her out to relieve herself. She searched for just the right spot, peed and then made a circuit of the yard's perimeter. Once she learned where her boundaries were, I never had to correct her again.

A startled rabbit dashed from under an azalea bush and streaked across the yard. Magdala ran in pursuit until the rabbit left her jurisdiction, then looked to see if I had noticed how well she was doing her job. After five minutes or so, she was satisfied that everything was under control and trotted back to the garage where I waited.

"Did anyone call and leave a message while I was out, Magdala?" I asked, closing the garage door. She looked at me and cocked her head, then seeing that I apparently did not expect anything of her, went to her water bowl and noisily slurped a drink.

My departmental cell phone rang and I answered it. "Tempest here."

"Congratulations, Chief Tempest, on solving Jerry Carpenter's murder. I knew you could do it," Ron Oxendine said.

"Making an arrest and getting a conviction are too different things, Ron. I still need your statement to tie this thing up."

"I don't see how I can help you," he said.

"You already did, Ron. *Cherchez la femme* you said this morning, then eliminated one of the two women Jerry was involved with. I bluffed Sadie and told her an eyewitness put Jerry at Sammy's Place that night. And I was right, wasn't I Ron?"

There was a long silence. For a moment I thought the call had been dropped. "You're right, Chief. I suppose I'm so used to dealing with stupid people, I forget that not everyone *is* stupid. I was watching when they left Sammy's Place that night."

"Without you to put Jerry Carpenter with Sadie that night, we may not have enough evidence to convict her."

"You wouldn't shuck and jive me would you, Chief?"

"If I thought it would help, I'd tap-dance in black face, but I don't have to. You can do the math. You gave me a clue and Sadie's in jail now. Besides, I'm still holding those DNA results for you."

"All right, Chief. I'll give you a statement, I've missed a lot of classes already," he replied. "I need to get back to school."

"When may I expect you, Ron?"

"You may expect me when you see me." Oxendine said just before the phone went dead.

"Magdala, somehow I don't think Ron Oxendine is getting into the spirit of cooperation I had hoped for," I said, putting the cell phone back in my pocket.

The German Shepherd's ears went up until she determined I didn't require anything of her. Then she went to the cabinet where I kept her dog food and stared at the doors intently.

"You're ready to eat, huh?" I opened the cabinet. "What will it be, Magdala? We have lamb and rice and sirloin flavor, to be served over the crunchy stuff."

Magdala sighed deeply to indicate she had no preference and was tired of waiting. "All right, then. Lamb and rice it is." She stood back patiently and waited as I put dry dog food in her dish and covered it with a small can of wet dog food. "Try not to wolf your food," I said.

"Something smells really good," Jennifer said, as she closed the garage door to the kitchen and kicked off her shoes as usual. There was a small, plastic shopping bag under her arm. "It's good to see you too, Magdala." The German Shepherd, licked her hand, sniffing at the bag, then went back to her usual spot by the table

"It's boneless pork loin and cornbread dressing, with asparagus and cranberry sauce on the side," I said. I slaved for every bit of a half hour."

"Let me change into something more comfortable," Jennifer said. "I have a gift someone asked me to deliver to you."

"I'll dish up the grub," I said.

"Be right back," she answered. Magdala trotted down the hallway after her. An unopened bag was her business as chief of security. Besides, there might be a treat for Magdala in an unopened bag. Our dog is an optimist.

The food was on the table and I was pouring our coffee when Jennifer came back in a deep green housecoat. Magdala was still on her heels, curiosity unsatisfied. Jennifer handed me the bag: "Open it before we eat."

"Your wish is my command," I replied.

By the weight and shape, I could tell it was a cup of some kind before I took it out of the bag. Once I had collected coffee mugs and occasionally a friend would still send me one. Usually they had a badge or other police insignia.

The mug from the bag, however, was exquisite. It was a swirl of light and dark clays with a transparent glaze. It made me think of the primal Earth itself, captured in motion.

"It's beautiful," I said, turning it over in my hands.

"Jorge Chávez made it. He brought it by the office and asked me to give it to you, with respect and admiration."

"Is he a ceramicist? This cup is first rate work."

"He was an apprentice pottery maker in Mexico. His father ran a small pottery operation until he died. Jorge's mother died when he was a baby, and his father was in debt. When his father died, the men he owed the money to tried to essentially turn Jorge into a slave in what had been his father's shop.

"Jorge heard that pottery-making was a valuable skill in this country, so he ran away. He managed to buy a small wheel and kiln, but he's had to support himself any way possible. I knew you'd appreciate the cup. He dug the clay from the banks of the Tennessee River."

"Does Jorge know I have friends in the ceramics business?"

"No, Shiloh. It was a *spontaneous* gift. I didn't even know he had this tremendous talent until he brought the cup in today," Jennifer said, taking a sip of coffee. She shook her head and scowled. "What police work does to the mind is horrible."

"I can't argue with that. We always look for the wheel turning within the wheel. I'll speak to someone about Jorge. He shouldn't be bussing tables."

"I thought you might. What's that delicious smell from the pork loin," she asked.

"Just a little cumin, pepper and garlic salt," I replied.

"Did you do this from a recipe?"

"No, I was just playing with spices, Jen. It's not much different from writing a story. A dash of this, a pinch of that."

"And both talents are a total mystery to me, Shiloh. My domain is the verifiable fact and the obvious precedent. Speaking of which, I saw on the news that you found Jerry Carpenter's murderer."

"We made an arrest," I said, taking a bite of pork loin and dressing. The asparagus was for Jennifer.

"You don't sound too convinced." She took a bite of meat, chewed, swallowed and said "This pork is spectacular, Shiloh."

"Jen, I'm never convinced until every scrap of evidence is in and every statement has been checked out. Sadie Hyde's partner in crime is on the run and Ron Oxendine has not told us what he knows."

"But you had probable cause for an arrest?" Jen paused with a bite of asparagus on her fork.

"Yes, we had probable cause. Sadie Hyde didn't fold, though, and try to help herself when we confronted her with the evidence. *That's* unusual."

"I'm sure you'll get to the bottom of it," she said. "I also brought you a gift, today,"

"And when do I get that gift?" I asked

"Right after I shower and get ready for bed," she took a bite of pork and dressing and closed her eyes. "Hmmmm. Eating delicious food is such a *sensua*l act."

"You didn't buy edible panties, did you?"

"Of course not. Don't you remember what a mess it made the last time? I had to shower again to get the gunk off."

"How about edible massage oil?" I asked.

"If you *must* know, I bought a copy of *Stakeout*. I thought we'd watch it together and see if Madeline Stowe's ass looked as good as mine."

"You devious, little minx," I said. "You always know how to make me an offer I can't refuse."

"I know. That's why I'm a superb trial attorney. You take Magdala out for her evening outing and I'll shower and set up the CD player. Just leave the dishes, I'll do them when I get up."

"You don't have to tell me twice. Let's take a walk, Magdala."

My dog ran to the door where her leash was hanging and waited expectantly. I picked up a small flashlight from the drawer beside the door. A leash was no longer needed, even at night.

Outside, we walked around to the back and Magdala made her evening check of the yard's perimeter. She stopped by the stand of trees in the very back and paused, lifting her nose into the air, then trotted on. Her stop had drawn my attention, though. I threw the halogen beam of the flashlight in that direction and thought I saw movement.

I knew it was unlikely that Magdala had passed so close to a prowler without noticing, but it was possible, if the wind was blowing towards him. German Shepherds don't track like bloodhounds, but with heads up, sniffing for crushed grass and disturbed soil.

Stopped short of the big tree where I had seen the movement, I cautiously looked behind it. There was nobody there — but I quickly discovered it was because he had moved while I was walking in that direction.

The club, which I later found to be a Louisville Slugger baseball bat, a professional model made of ash and painted black, whistled by my head with the first swing. I was backing up, trying to draw my weapon when he swung the second time and hit my left arm above the elbow, instantly numbing it.

I twisted away, almost clearing my holster, when the third swing hit me directly across the chest, driving out the wind and making me instantly aware of the defibrillator buried in my lower chest.

I went down, dropping my pistol and telling my body to roll into a ball, but my body didn't respond. The dark figure stood over me and I knew the next blow would fall on my head. And it would have, except that a snarling Magdala streaked over me, a low rumble coming from her chest, and knocked my assailant to the ground. I heard him grunt in pain as she sank her teeth into him.

He got up, and tried to run with Magdala grabbing his leg, snarling. I managed to get out one word, fearing that he would seriously hurt my German Shepherd. "*Magdala*!"

Instantly she returned and licked my face. I could hear the man crashing through the stand of trees as he escaped. "Good girl, Magdala. Good girl!" I could barely get out my words and my breathing was labored. Magdala looked into my face, whimpered, then ran towards the house.

Drifting in and out, unaware of how much time had passed, I heard Jennifer's voice as from a distance.

"Shiloh, Jesus can't you walk the dog without getting into a lethal battle? Yes," I heard her say, realizing that she was on her cell phone. "This is Jennifer Mendoza." She reeled off our address and gave the information she knew would most quickly mobilize all emergency services. "Officer down, needs emergency medical assistance and back-up! It's Chief Shiloh Tempest. Someone tried to kill him and he's unconscious."

Jennifer closed the phone and got down beside me. "Shiloh, can you hear me?"

"Yes," I managed to say in a sort of hiss.

"I had just stepped out of the shower when Magdala came to the door and started throwing herself against it, barking. I opened the kitchen door and she had a bloody froth around her mouth. Then she turned and ran back out here. Are you stabbed or cut?"

"Clubbed," I said. "Baseball bat, I think. The blood belonged to the guy who attacked me. Magdala saved my life."

Hearing her name, Magdala licked my cheek and whimpered.

"I guess Magdala decided that turn about is fair play. The last time you saved her," Jennifer said.

My breath was coming back in short spurts. Apparently the defibrillator had not been damaged. "Jen, I hear sirens. Why don't you go put on a robe. You're stark naked and wet."

"Will you be all right?" she asked.

"Yeah, Magdala will stay with me."

"All right, I'll be right back."

She ran to the house and darted into the garage just before the ambulance and first police car pulled up. I was smiling to myself despite the pain. How many women would run outside naked to help a lover — and have the presence of mind to grab a cell phone?

Twenty-one

My eyelids felt as if they were sticking together, but I finally managed to open them. I had slept hard after the Demerol shot in the emergency room. Every time it began to wear off, someone gave me another and I floated away again.

"Hey, Hoss, do I need to assign you a bodyguard?" Sheriff Sam Renfro was sitting by my bed, wearing a wrinkled tan suit, buckskin shoes and a pink tie, loose at the neck over a pearl gray shirt. He had become a sharp dresser since being appointed Sheriff.

"No thanks, the one I have now does a pretty good job."

"That she did. There was a lot of blood on the Louisville Slugger ball bat someone tried to take you out with. Looks like it might have been purchased for that very purpose. It's new and I've got Al Reagan and John Freed trying to find out where it was purchased.

"No prints on the bat, but we got plenty of DNA for comparison and a size ten and a half footprint with a fairly unique pattern. Got a detective working that angle, too."

"Sam, you don't need to put half my detectives on an assault," I said.

"Assault hell! It was the attempted murder of a police officer. You know we don't let that slide, Shy. By the way, how do you feel?"

"It hurts to breathe, but other than that I feel okay. Since I didn't have surgery, I take it the implanted defibrillator wasn't damaged, Sam. And where is Jennifer?"

"Negative on the surgery. I sent Jen down to get coffee and something to eat. I had never seen her take charge like she did last night. Another ideal of feminine reticence bites the dust.

"She was barking orders and even the doctors were listening, Shy. Jen was a sight to see — like a mother lion watching over her cubs.

"Shy, I don't suppose you got a look at the guy who tried to take you out. Jen said you didn't mention a name before they shot you full of Schedule II narcotics."

"He was probably wearing a ski mask because I don't remember seeing any features, and he never spoke — just grunted when Magdala grabbed him. I can tell you he was a good six inches taller than I am, but most men are."

"Looks like he knew what he was doing," Sam said.

"No, Sam, I was almost killed by an amateur. I did everything but walk up there and point a flashlight at myself. A pro would've killed me before I had a chance to kill him. If I'd had my weapon out, he'd be dead. Definitely an amateur."

"You don't really expect it to happen at home," Sam said. "And I know this is a silly question, but can you think of anyone who might want to kill you?"

A second later, we both burst out laughing and it definitely hurt my sore ribs. Asking any real kick-ass cop if there's anyone who might want to see him dead is ludicrous. We *all* have people who would like to see us dead. It's an occupational hazard.

"Damn, Sheriff! I almost passed out on that bit of humor. It hurts to laugh when you've been worked over by a Louisville Slugger."

"Catch your breath, then answer the question. Are you working anything now that might have brought wrath down on you? Maybe not on your regular job, but possibly on the Jerry Carpenter case."

"There's one man who's actually a suspect in Jerry's murder case. His name's Ron Oxendine. But I can pretty well assure you that it wasn't him that clubbed me last night."

"How can you be sure?" Sam asked.

"Because I have information he wants very badly and because I'd be dead if he had decided to kill me."

"You think he's *that* dangerous, Shy?"

"It's the same man who disarmed two KPD investigators and then slipped through the fingers of our SWAT team, Sam. I figure him for ex-Delta Force."

"Always with the business talk," Jennifer said, coming through the door with two cups of coffee in a cardboard holder from the cafeteria. "Why do I never catch you two discussing football or women like ordinary redneck men? Welcome back, Chief Tempest." She leaned over and kissed me lightly.

"Did you bring me coffee?" I asked.

"Of course, I did. Brought you and your friend the Sheriff a cup."

"Now, if I had a woman like Jen to wake up to, I'd be content," Sam said.

"Bull, Sam Renfro," Jennifer said, "the idea of being with the same woman more than a week sends you into a panic."

"Jen, you have no idea how much that hurts, but you're probably right," Sam said. "And now that Shy's in the land of the living, I think I'll bid the two of you, adieu."

"Thanks for coming by, Sam — even if it was just to leer at Jennifer," I said.

"We do appreciate your presence at times like this, Sam," Jennifer said, kissing him on the cheek. "And you should come to dinner. I have a young female associate in my office who is a lot like me."

"On that note, I am gone." Sam said.

"He needs a woman to straighten him out," Jennifer said as the door closed behind Sam.

"Don't hold your breath," I said. "He tried marriage once and didn't like it."

"On a more pressing note, do you know who tried to kill you, Shiloh?"

"We'll probably know when the results come back from forensics. Thanks to Magdala, he left a lot of DNA in the form of blood."

"What about the gut feeling you men always talk about? Don't you have a gut feeling about who tried to knock your brains out with a Louisville Slugger?"

"Jennifer, I've racked up a long list of people who wouldn't mind seeing me dead. I've outlived a lot of them. The evidence will tell the story."

"You men also have a testosterone impairment," Jennifer said. "And very often it leads to an early death."

She had a point, so I didn't try to argue with her.

My encounter with a baseball bat only kept me away from work two days. Back in the office I sat down to reduce my backlog of phone calls and messages. The biggest was a complaint from a woman who had accused one of my detectives of fondling her. It was the second such complaint in two weeks.

A cop is an easy target for people trying to collect a quick nuisance settlement, but it was unusual to have two so close together in a department the size of KCSO.

Sam had placed my detective on paid suspension and sent a copy of the complaint to my office and the Internal Affairs Division. They had a two day head start on me in IAD, but I knew they would have spent that time interviewing the complainant and looking at the detective's personnel file. I decided to actually investigate.

It took Al Reagan and John Freed exactly two hours to find, not one but two similar complaints from the same woman. The first complaint had been against a Knoxville Police Department patrol officer and the second against a Blount County detective.

Both cases had been investigated by the Tennessee Bureau of Investigation and the respective attorney generals' offices and found to be bogus. In addition, she had filed fondling complaints against medical personnel in a Blount County mental health facility on one of several stays there. I copied the reports and hand carried them to IAD.

I knocked and heard Sergeant Black tell me to come in. I opened the door and saw that he was alone. "Where's the other half of the Black and White squad?"

"Sergeant White is on vacation," Black said, running his finger around the inside of his collar. "How can I help you?"

"You have a complaint on one of my detectives. Have you done an investigation yet."

"Which detective would that be?" Black asked.

"I'm not in the mood for your horseshit today, Black. There's only one detective under suspension and I need him back at work."

"He will be back to work or terminated when I have time to investigate, *thoroughly*. You know the drill, Chief."

"Yes, I do know the drill, at least the way it's done by your office. You hang an officer out to dry the way you did John Freed and let him sweat it out for days or weeks. But, if you hadn't noticed, there's a new sheriff in town."

I pitched the folder on Black's desk. "Here's enough to close the case and it took all of two hours to find it. I'm going to turn this evidence over to Sam Renfro and I'd suggest you get *your* report in before another day passes."

"I'm not in your chain of command," Black said.

"You'd better be glad you're not because I would have you investigating vandalism complaints or working as a school crossing guard, Black. I'll expect my detective back tomorrow. I'm going to call and tell him he's been cleared so he can sleep tonight."

Black's face turned a bright shade of pink. "I'll have a look at your file as soon as possible, Chief Tempest."

"See that you do, Sergeant Black. Keep your seat. I can find my own way out."

When I returned to my office, Tom Abernathy was standing in front of my door, talking to Al Reagan. They grew silent as I entered the squad room. "Come on in, gentlemen, and have a seat."

In my office, we all settled in and leaned back in our chairs. "What character flaw of mine were you two discussing when I came in?"

"Reagan here tells me you may be leaving in a few days, Chief," Abernathy said. "I'd hate to see that happen — especially in light of the fact that I'm up on insubordination charges. I may be looking for a job shortly."

"Whether I stay or not is still undecided. To whom were you insubordinate?"

"Hodge tried to pull me off the Jerry Carpenter case and I threatened to go public. The bastard was going to give the case to Claiborne. He cited a lack of progress and accused me of allowing you to run the investigation," Abernathy said.

"You just made an arrest," I said. "Where does he get the idea that there's a lack of progress?"

"He said if I'd been on my toes, Ralph Ogg would have been in custody, not on the run. You know how Hodge is."

"Hodge sounds like somebody Reagan used to work for," I said.

"That true, Tom. But Chief Tempest was kind enough to shoot him. A good supervisor is a pearl without price," Reagan said.

"How serious do you think Hodge is, Tom?" I asked.

"I don't think he'll try to fire me, but I can see myself walking a beat in the Old City," Abernathy replied.

"Then I guess we'd better wrap this up soon," I said.

Twenty-two

Catching up always takes more out of me than working a case. By three o'clock, I was dragging and my ribs were hurting, so I decided to call it a day and get out of the downtown area before the traffic really got bad.

Ten minutes later I made a right turn off Hill Avenue and drove up the hill to the red-light at Main, across the street from the old main post office, where the military recruiters had once had their offices in the basement. It was where I had enlisted in the Army in 1965 on my eighteenth birthday. Today, the real postal center is out west, where most other things are.

A left turn on Cumberland, took me to Henley Street, from which the Sunsphere was clearly visible behind the new convention center.

All the points of a man's life criss-cross in numerous places when he chooses to live where he was born. I had left Knoxville several times, but always returned. My son, Micah, is just past thirty-four and is currently in Charlotte — not having yet learned where home is. Because of his vindictive mother, he and I haven't had a smooth relationship.

My cell phone piped out the notes of *The Sting*, jarring me from my thoughts. "This is Tempest," I said.

"Chief Tempest, are you ready to take my statement?"

"I didn't notice you in my office, Ron. I'm on my way home."

"Can you cut a little slack for a military man who has a few demons about being trapped, Chief?"

"Ron, I've already cut you a lot of slack because you're a military vet. It's becoming a little tiresome.

"If you don't come in, we're going to charge you with aggravated assault. We probably can't find you, but you'll never be able to come home either. I think that's important to you."

"I'll make a statement that I saw Sadie and Jerry leave Sammy's together that night. I know you have that little recorder with you. What difference does it make *where* I talk to you?

"I just need a little reassurance that I'm not a suspect any longer. I'll testify at the trial."

For a few moments I was silent. I remembered how I had been when I first came home from Vietnam — half-crazy with guilt and rage. "All right, Ron. Where do you want to meet?"

"Just drive and I'll call you back when you get off on I-275 on your way home. I'll be close by."

Before I could respond, he broke the connection. I thought about Abernathy's warning. "*That boy has been places where none of us have ever been,*" Tom had warned me. But was it true? When you kill your first man, isn't that as far as any of us can go?

Five minutes later, as I was exiting I-275, Ron Oxendine called again. "Yes, Ron?" I said.

"Turn right on Emory and drive until I tell you to pull into a location I've chosen," he said.

"It had better be close, Ron. I'm aching all over and I'm tired." It was obvious he was tracking me, but he could have tracked me any time he wanted and if my death was his eventual goal, that would be easy enough for him. Why would he want to kill me, though?

As I neared the intersection of Emory and Norris Freeway, my cell phone once more played *The Sting*. "Chief, pull into the parking lot of Beaver Dam Baptist Church, around back. Wait for me."

A couple of minutes later, I was sitting on the parking lot of Beaver Dam Baptist Church, which has grown into what's called a megaplex. It was big, even when I was a high school student across the street at Halls High School.

In those days, high school students had a smoking circle and would walk down to the church after school to settle disagreements with fisticuffs and nobody cared in the adult world.

There were a few kids playing behind the church but they paid me no mind. After ten minutes, I took my phone, called up the number of Oxendine's cell phone and punched it in. There was no answer. I sighed deeply and started the car.

Apparently, Oxendine had seen something that made him nervous and decided not to make the meet. Paranoia is a sad thing and a part of every violent profession.

At home, I parked my maroon cruiser in the driveway, leaving room for Jennifer to get in on her side of the garage. I noticed that the grass needed mowing at least one more time before fall. Keeping up a house is hard work, but Jennifer had grown up in apartments and the house was a sign of stability for her.

I unlocked the garage door and stepped in. Immediately, I knew something was wrong because Magdala was not scratching at the entrance to the kitchen. But the realization was too late in coming.

"Just relax, Chief," Ron Oxendine said. "I'm not here to do any harm. I just had to make sure I wasn't walking into a trap."

"Ron, it's hard to relax when your home has just been invaded," I said.

"Chief, I could have gone in, but then I would have had to hurt your dog. It's a smart dog and a big dog. I heard it sniffing quietly under the door. It knows I'm here and yet it has remained quiet. No barking at all."

"I appreciate small favors, Ron."

"Don't let your anger get the best of you, Chief. I just want my answer. Then I'll give you the taped statement."

"Ron, are you aware of how deep your paranoia runs?"

"Chief, you of all people should know that just because you're paranoid doesn't mean people aren't out to get you. Hand your pistol to me, butt first, without turning around."

I did as he said because I had no viable choice. "Ron, you weren't just Delta were you? You did wet work, didn't you?"

"Chief, when you carry weapons for a living, it's *all* wet work. Now, what are we going to do so that your dog doesn't get hurt?"

"I'll lock her in the bedroom," I said.

"If she gets away from you, I won't have a choice," Oxendine said.

"You had a choice not to break into my home — but I'll make sure she doesn't attack," I said.

"Do it, Chief. I hope you won't force me to shoot either of you. I admire courage, but it won't keep me from doing what I have to do."

"I'm going to open the door. The bedroom is a straight walk down the hall from the kitchen."

"All right, Chief. I'll be right behind you."

I opened the door a crack. "Magdala, back!"

Her hair was standing up on the back of her neck and her teeth were pulled back over her teeth, but she backed up from the door and I stepped in and caught her by the collar.

"Good girl, Magdala. This way, go with me. Before turning, she looked at Ron Oxendine with pure malevolence in her pale amber eyes and a rumble came from her chest. Nonetheless, she went with me inside the bedroom.

"Sit, Magdala. Stay!" I stepped back quickly and closed the door. Magdala immediately began to scratch at the door and whimper.

"That's a fine dog, Chief. I'm backing away. You can face me, but don't make any sudden moves. When we get to the kitchen, walk by me. I will back up to the wall behind the kitchen table. I made coffee for you the last time we met. Will you return the favor?"

"Sure, Ron. Let's do it," I said.

In the kitchen, Oxendine placed himself with his back to the wall and sat down in one of the chairs. "We've done well so far, Chief. Start the coffee. I trust you have my letter. Do you have a cassette recorder in the house or do we need to get one from your car?"

"I have one in that drawer." I pointed to the top drawer over the cabinet where I kept my pots and pans.

"Back up to the door, Chief." For the first time I saw that he was holding a Glock pistol, probably a .40 caliber. My smaller Glock was tucked in his belt.

He opened the drawer and looked in, his pistol trained on me. "You *do* have a recorder in here. I thought maybe it was a pistol." He took the recorder out, stepped back and put it on the table. "Maybe you're not as paranoid as I am, Chief."

"I have to get the coffee down from the shelf over the stove," I said.

"Do it, but do it slowly. If you make me nervous, I'll kill you and then go in there and kill Magdala. Where did you come up with that name?"

"She already was Magdala when I got her." I slowly took down the coffee can and took the lid off slowly. I put a fresh filter in the coffee maker and cautiously put in three scoops of dark Colombian coffee, then filled the reservoir with water and turned on the brewing cycle.

"How long, Chief?"

"About five minutes," I said. "I want you out before Jennifer gets home."

"How long, Chief?"

"A couple of hours."

"Shouldn't be a problem unless I have to kill you — if you get my drift."

"Loud and clear, Ron. The DNA results are inside my jacket pocket. I'd like to take it off, anyway. It's warm in here."

"Pull the jacket open with your left hand and let me see the envelope."

I did as he told me.

"Now, take the envelope out with the index finger and thumb of your right hand — slowly," he said.

I removed the envelope and slid it across the table.

"All right, stand up and remove the jacket, beginning with the right arm, and hand it to me," Oxendine said. "Then raise your trousers above your ankles. Good."

When the jacket was in his hands, he laid it on the table and patted it. Satisfied that it was safe, he pulled the envelope across the table towards him.

"Are you going to look at the results of the DNA test?" I asked.

"Coffee first, Chief. Why don't you get it ready, ever so slowly. Don't screw it up at this point. We're almost done."

Rising slowly, I turned, walked to the cabinet and took down two mugs. "How do you drink your coffee, Jerry? Black like the coffee you gave me at your house?"

"Yes, black and hot, Chief," he replied, staring directly into my eyes. He was young, his face largely unlined — younger than my own son. His eyes were a pale amber, like those of a jungle cat.

I had sadly misjudged Ron Oxendine. He was not a troubled soldier, trying to recover from the stress of combat. His defect had been with him when he was recruited for wet work. The military watches psychological evaluations. What we call normal does not apply to those who become good assassins.

The difference between what we call a serial killer in police work and an assassin is nothing more than a government sanction. They are psychopaths, and even their handlers avoid them except when absolutely necessary. Nobody knows what robs a human being of his soul, but it happens. Some are lacking the thing that makes us human; that thing is empathy.

Theories come and go, but nobody really knows what produces people like Ron Oxendine — or Ted Bundy or the Son of Sam. A current theory is that they never bond with their mothers or anyone else at a critical point in their infancy.

Ron's mother had been a drug addict, unlikely to have offered much to an infant, but like all the other theories, it is just that.

Men and women without empathy exist. That we do know for sure.

I poured the first cup of coffee, then as I moved to pour the next, the pot slipped and I scalded my left hand. As I stepped away, shaking the hot liquid off my hand, Ron Oxendine rose from his seat, the pistol pointed at my chest. I knew I was a hair trigger from death. I slowly lifted my hands, palms out.

"Try to be careful, Chief Tempest. I almost killed you."

"I know. I'm going to put a lump of sugar in my coffee, then pick up both the cups and carry them to the table, Ron."

"Slow and steady, Chief."

I put a lump of sugar in my coffee, slowly opened the silverware drawer for a spoon to stir it. I laid down the spoon and picked up the two cups of coffee, being careful not to stumble. I put both cups down and took a seat across from Oxendine.

"Chief, it takes a lot of composure to put sugar in your coffee with a pistol pointed at you."

"I like my coffee the way I like it, Ron."

He smiled, picked up the coffee with his left hand and took a sip, never taking his eyes off me, the pistol perfectly steady. "Excellent coffee," he said. "Before you sit down, take your shirttail out, slowly — just in case you have something in your belt."

"I'm not hiding another piece on me, Ron." Nonetheless, I complied.

"Okay, Chief. Take a seat, slowly!"

I sat down, took a sip, savored it, and said: "The coffee maker did most of the work."

"Do you want me to check the DNA results, or do you want to interview me first?" Oxendine asked.

"Let's get the interview out of the way, Ron."

"Turn on the recorder and let's do it," he said.

Turning on the recorder, I gave the date, time and location, then said: "Present for this interview are Ronald James Oxendine and myself, Chief of Detectives Shiloh Tempest of the Knox County Sheriff's Office.

"Mister Oxendine, you have the right to remain silent and

the right to the presence of an attorney before questioning. Even if you begin talking, you may stop and ask for an attorney at any time. Should you give up these rights, anything you say may be used against you in a court of law. Do you understand your rights?"

"Very thorough, Chief. Yes, I understand my rights and I'm voluntarily answering questions."

"On the evening when Jerry Carpenter was killed, did you have occasion to observe anything at Sammy's Place on Clinton Highway?"

"Yes. I was parked across the street from Sammy's Place, waiting for Jerry Carpenter to arrive. We'd had an argument and I was going to apologize."

"Tell me what happened while you were waiting," I said.

"Jerry pulled into the lot and got out of his truck, carrying what looked like a sword from where I was. He tried to carry it inside, but was denied entrance by the bouncer. Then Sadie came out, talked to Jerry and went back in.

"A couple of minutes later, she came back out in street clothes. She and Jerry left in his truck with her driving — probably because she thought Jerry was too drunk to drive."

"Did you ever see Jerry alive again?"

"No, I did not."

"That concludes the interview. It is now 4:55 p.m."

"That's *it*?" Oxendine said.

"That's it," I replied. "Another cup of coffee, Ron?"

"Sure," he said. "Why did you insist on having me come in for an interview? You had enough to put away Sadie and the pinhead without me, didn't you?"

"Procedure, Ron. The law requires procedure." I picked up his cup and mine, went to the counter and poured two cups.

"Actually," I said, "Sadie broke off one of her green, fake fingernails at the World's Fair site. With the rest of what we had, it was enough, but I needed your corroboration."

"She broke off a fake nail? Did she leave enough real nail to get a DNA sample?" Oxendine asked.

"She sure did, Ron," I lied.

"So with the two cigarette butts that Tiny smoked and the DNA from Sadie, you tied them both to the scene?" He smiled. "That was really dumb on their part."

"That it was, Ron. Of course, I had no way of knowing *you* were there until you told me about Tiny smoking the two cigarettes. *Don't* try to pick your weapon up, Ron! I have a .44 special pistol pointed at your chest under the table."

His fingers twitched but he didn't try to pick up the Glock. Our eyes locked. "Are you trying to bluff me, Chief?"

"I don't do bluffs, Ron."

"Even if you do have a .44 pistol aimed at my chest, I'm fast enough that I'll probably get off rounds."

"You might, Ron, but you won't be around to kill my dog or threaten Jennifer.

"That became my central concern the moment you made the threat. I don't expect you to understand that I'm willing to die because I love Jennifer and Magdala more than my own life. It's an alien concept to you and your kind."

"What *is* my kind, Chief?"

"You're a wanton killer, Ron. You killed Jerry Carpenter because you *thought* he was your father and blamed him for whatever's wrong with you. You tried to frame Osteen and now you're trying to frame two other people for what you did."

"If you *do* have a pistol, and I don't know that I believe it, where was it?" Oxendine asked.

"It was in a holster attached to the underside of the table. You underestimated *my* paranoia, Ron. There was a snub-nosed Colt .38 special by the coffee can in the cabinet. I didn't go for it then because I was pretty sure you'd get me before I got you — and I *believed* you'd kill Magdala, then wait on Jennifer.

"I knew the .44 was there and I only needed you to relax a little. I didn't kill you without warning because I'm not a killer by nature."

"Your predecessor as chief of detectives would disagree — if you hadn't killed him, Chief. You're as much of a killer as I am."

"No, I'm not. I'm a law enforcement officer. If you'll stand up, turn and put your hands against the wall, I'll call for back-up and have you transported to jail. You only die if you force me to kill you, Ron."

"I'm not going to jail, so I'll offer you a counter proposition. We both walk away alive. I take the tape and give my word that I'll disappear and never bother you or your loved ones again," he said.

"Sorry, Ron. I'm the police and we work for God. 'Thou shalt not kill.' You're under arrest for first degree murder."

"In that case," I saw his eyes flicker before his hand twitched, "I'll..."

The first .44 slug hit him directly under the heart, the second destroyed his sternum. I was moving by that time so none of the four rounds he got off hit me before my third round struck him high in the chest.

He leaned back against the wall, staring at me as if in disbelief. His Glock pistol slipped from his hand as he slid down the wall, leaving a swath of blood. I took my cell phone out and dialed 911.

"This is Knox County, Unit 4. Shots fired, suspect down. I need a first responder and an ambulance on the way to...."

My pistol had remained pointed at him the entire time I was on the phone. I stepped around the table and kicked his pistol away. I could hear the blood gurgling and wheezing though the sucking chest wound my pistol had caused, just below his throat.

"Ron," I got down on one knee beside him, "hang on. Help is on the way."

He turned his eyes towards my face. "You got me good, old Sky Soldier," he said, coughing up bloody foam.

"Don't talk, Ron. Help is on the way."

"Read me the results of the test, Chief." He coughed up another mouthful of bloody foam. "Last request and all that," he wheezed.

I reached up on the table, got the envelope and tore it open. I looked at it closely and it said what I knew it would. Jerry Carpenter and Ron Oxendine were not related.

"Whas' it say, Chief?" Blood had begun to bubble through his nose and the rattling in his chest was growing louder.

"Ron, it says..." Before I could get the words out, Oxendine coughed up what looked like a large clot of blood and closed his eyes for the last time. In the distance, I could hear a Rural Metro fire department first responder coming up the side of the small mountain on which I live.

I stood up, tossed the DNA results on the kitchen table, now splintered where I had shot through it to kill Ron Oxendine. I reached over and turned off the tape recorder I had left running, then went back to the bedroom to try and calm Magdala down.

He had never learned that Jerry wasn't his father. I would probably never know what he did with Jerry's heart.

Epilogue

"Chief Tempest, you got a minute?" Al Reagan asked from outside my office door.

"Sure, Al. I have time for you and your skinny, redheaded sidekick, any time." He and John Freed came in and stood in front of my desk.

"There were two baseball bats like the one used to work you over sold at a high-end sports store down in West Knoxville the week before you were attacked. We tracked down the first one and it had no traces of blood on it. In fact, it had never been used," Freed said in his near-falsetto voice.

"The second Louisville Slugger was purchased by Roy Jamison, the guy you arrested for abusing your German Shepherd, Magdala. The thing is, Jamison's National Guard unit was called up and sent to Iraq a couple of days after you were attacked.

"On a felony, where we have DNA, the Army will send him home for us to deal with. Do you want us to pull him in? If we don't test his DNA, we'll probably never make the case."

I leaned back in my chair and looked at them for a moment. "Why don't we leave Jamison where he is. Maybe he'll redeem himself in Iraq."

"If he gets killed..." Reagan began.

"Then he's out of our jurisdiction," I said.

"Don't you want to *know*, Chief ?" Reagan asked.

"Al, I'm pretty sure I already know. Maybe Jamison will come back a man; maybe he'll look me up and apologize," I said.

"You feeling okay, Chief?" Freed asked.

"What the hell is this?" Sam Renfro said, coming through my office door. "Don't you detectives have anything else to do except stand around?"

"Gosh, Sheriff, we were just giving the chief an update," Freed said, becoming flustered.

"Freed, I'm joking," Sam said. "You need to lighten up, son. How are you doing, Al?"

"I'm good, Sheriff. How about you?"

"I'm *great*!" Sam said. "I have something for you, though." Sam handed Al Reagan a shiny, new lieutenant's badge. "With Shy being short a lieutenant and with him being on mandatory suspension pending investigation on the psychopath he blew away two days ago, I decided I needed a lieutenant.

For the time being, you're an *acting* lieutenant. Of course, that gives you a leg up when interviews begin."

"Sheriff, I appreciate this," Reagan said, seemingly stunned, "but whether or not I bid on the lieutenant's job still depends on whether Chief Tempest stays as chief of detectives."

"Not a problem, then," Sam said. "We put Chief Tempest's paperwork through this morning. He's back on the payroll."

"Gentlemen," I said, "no party. No celebration. You're the only ones who know right now. Let's keep it quiet."

"Gosh, Chief, I'm so happy I could bust," Freed's voice choked.

"Freed!" Sam said, "If you blubber I'll kick your ass."

"John's a little high-strung, Sheriff," Reagan said.

"Well, hell, there's no wonder," Sam said. "We have to take that boy out and teach him how to cuss! He needs to *ventilate* once in a while."

"In that case, drinks are on me," I said, "but the meal at Regas is on you, Sam."

"Then let's go," Sam said.

"Really?" Freed said.

"Would the High Sheriff lie, Freed? Let's go," Sam said.

As we were leaving my office, Tom Abernathy entered the squad room.

"You two know, Abernathy. Sheriff, this is Tom Abernathy, he was assigned to the Jerry Carpenter case. He's a first class cop. Tom, this is Sheriff Sam Renfro."

They shook hands. "Nice to meet you, Tom," the Sheriff said. "Did you need something before we go to lunch?"

The tall, Denzel Washington look-alike, smiled. "Nope, had some time on my hands and just came by to see Chief Tempest. I had the time because I'm on suspension for insubordination."

"And to whom were you insubordinate," I asked.

"My chief, Frank Hodge."

"In that case," Sam said, "you can go to lunch with us and tell us how Hodge turned purple when you talked back to him — if you don't mind eating with a cop who drinks Sprite and doesn't cuss."

"You mean Detective Freed?" Tom asked. "His courtesy is legendary."

"Come on, guys..." Freed began.

"Button it up, Freed," the sheriff said, "or I'll assign you to vice and you'll *have* to learn how to be as crude and vulgar as the rest of us."

There was a smile on my face as I walked to the garage among friends. Tomorrow would bring another case, another crisis, but today things were good.

Printed in the United States
203640BV00002B/265-345/P

9 781604 540017